'I admit people suffer—and I go through hell, too—but often it's the only way.'

He went through hell! Gabrielle's look chopped him into little pieces. Whoever lost out in a deal with Saul O'Connor, she was sure it would never be him.

'In other words, you've made a career out of being ruthless,' she accused, her tone curt with contempt. 'Isn't that a perfect example of fitting the man to the job!'

'Haven't you ever wondered if your view of the past could be faulty?' he demanded, as he pulled the BMW on to the parking-bay outside her offices. 'Hasn't it occurred to you that maybe I was not entirely the big bad wolf?'

'*Never*.' She used the word as incisively as a surgeon would use a scalpel.

Books you will enjoy
by ELIZABETH OLDFIELD

SPARRING PARTNERS
David Llewellyn made his low opinion of Shelly all too
clear. She travelled all the way to the tropical island of
Nevis to make him change his mind, but her efforts
seemed doomed to failure . . .

RENDEZVOUS IN RIO
Six months ago Christa had been forced to leave
Jefferson Barssi because of his arrogance and hard-
heartedness. Now she was forced to return—and he
didn't seem to have changed at all!

THE
PRICE OF
PASSION

BY

ELIZABETH OLDFIELD

MILLS & BOON LIMITED
ETON HOUSE   18-24 PARADISE ROAD
RICHMOND   SURREY   TW9 1SR

First published in Great Britain 1989 by Mills & Boon Limited

© Elizabeth Oldfield 1989

Australian copyright 1989 Philippine copyright 1990 This edition 1990

ISBN 0 263 76523 7

Set in English Times 11 on 12 pt. 01 – 9001 – 43890

Typeset in Great Britain by JCL Graphics, Bristol

Made and Printed in Great Britain

CHAPTER ONE

'SAUL O'CONNOR'S coming here *today*?' Gabrielle protested, in a voice suddenly as tight as piano wire.

'That's the message on the answering machine.'

'But his appointment with Betancourts was only confirmed last week!'

The burly, bespectacled young man who had followed her into her office gave a mild shrug. 'You read the newspapers, you know the guy's powerhouse reputation. He doesn't waste time. It's up at six-thirty, ten sets of tennis before breakfast, then he's off to knock big business into shape—excellent shape. Mind you, his tennis could've tailed off of late. Playing in sunny California is one thing, but——' Kevin Holland walked over to the floor-to-ceiling window which provided a bird's-eye view of the city '—smashing a ball around in London in winter is a very different proposition.'

At dawn it had begun to snow, and now fat, feathery flakes were tumbling from a leaden February sky. Far below, roofs, domes and spires were layered white, while a treacherous mix of black ice and frozen mush had turned the streets into skating-rinks. Whether on wheels or on foot, progressing from A to B was a matter of skid, slide and considerable luck.

'Unless he's become a member of some exclusive sports club with indoor courts,' Gabrielle muttered, sitting down behind her desk to unzip and pull off knee-high black leather boots.

'Which is more than likely. Our new chief executive's the kind of individual who makes things happen—same as you.' Her companion grinned. 'Come to think of it, you two have a heck of a lot in common.'

'No, we do not!'

'OK, you're the entrepreneurial type while O'Connor's more of a corporate animal,' Kevin amended, too busy yodelling his song of praise to notice the heat of her denial. 'For someone of only thirty-five, he's logged some spectacular successes. First he put Meyers Land back on the road to health. Next he was enticed across the Atlantic to work wonders with that property corporation. And last year he performed miracles with——'

'Saul O'Connor did start off with one or two advantages,' she cut in tartly, 'and for your information he's thirty-six. He had a birthday last month.'

Kevin looked impressed. 'You *do* read the papers.'

A wisp of copper-gold had escaped the confines of the sleek knot of hair at the nape of her neck, and Gabrielle frowned as she skewered it back into place.

'The burglar-alarm man mixed up his dates and

instead of next Monday he appeared this morning, which is why I'm late,' she said, in a swift change of subject. 'I told him it wasn't convenient, but he insisted on taking me through a long demonstration of which button relates to what.' She pulled a face. 'The system's so complicated, I stopped listening after the first five minutes.'

'You did set the alarm before you left? You must,' Kevin insisted, when she shook her head. 'You've moved into an extremely affluent neighbourhood.'

'No one's going to lust after a haphazard collection of second-hand furniture and some tea-chests filled with dishwasher-safe cups and saucers!'

'But the thieves won't know what your worldly goods comprise until after they've broken in,' he pointed out with grave and indisputable logic.

Gabrielle ignored him. Kevin could be horribly mundane at times.

'Garden of Eden Mews, the Royal Borough of Kensington, London West Eight,' she chanted, picturing the tranquil cobbled backwater. Originally stables in the eighteen hundreds, the buildings had been converted into an assortment of *bijoux* residences—terracotta houses, glass-and-aluminium studios, ivy-clad cottages. With its window-boxes and the Victorian gas-lights beside the porch, Number seven was one of the prettiest. The dimples in her cheeks deepened. 'I never imagined I'd live anywhere so chic, so central, so gorgeous.'

'One happy Eve. All you need now is an Adam. Not me,' Kevin hastened to assure her, when wary green eyes swung his way. Long ago he had attempted to pay court and been firmly, though kindly, rebuffed. Nothing personal, it was simply a case of her not having the time to give a close relationship the attention it would require. But please, Gabrielle had begged, could they continue to be friends? They could. They were. 'However, you are twenty-seven and, as they say, the meter is running.'

Her feet slid into classic court shoes. 'You sound just like my mother. That there are twelve Anniversaries shops in prime London locations making major buckeroos doesn't impress her one jot. All she wants is to see me walk down the aisle or, preferably, gallop.'

'I expect she's keen to have grandchildren.'

'She's desperate!' A shadow clouded her face and for a moment she was quiet, then Gabrielle briskly drew the swivel-chair up to her desk. Buried beneath a mass of reports, sales catalogues and samples of everything from porcelain orchids to marzipan pigs to aluminium pens shaped like space rockets, it gave evidence of a mind too active to be overly concerned with tidiness. 'Did Saul O'Connor quote a time for his visitation?' she enquired.

'Ten-thirty.'

Her eyes flew to the chunky gold watch on her wrist. 'But that's in half an hour!' she protested, grabbing the telephone which had given a sudden squeal.

Countless calls were the norm for her day—the first batch being made and received before she ever reached the office—and this one came from a manufacturer of cashmere socks. Prices were discussed, discounts argued, a high-speed deal struck.

'Apparently our new overlord's decided to kick off with a whistle-stop tour of the more accessible parts of the conglomerate,' Kevin said, as she dumped the receiver and began separating papers into hasty piles. He pushed the thick-framed spectacles further up his nose. 'It's nothing to get jumpy about.'

'I'm not jumpy! Why should I be? It's just that once . . .' Her voice trailed away. As far as Kevin was concerned—as far as *everyone* was concerned—she was the woman with the sparkling present and future, so why spoil things by owning up to a murky past? Revelations at this late stage were pointless. 'Anniversaries doesn't need knocking into shape,' she said, fixating on business. 'You're the accountant, and if anyone knows how profitable we are, you do. We're streamlined, efficient——'

'Gabrielle, Mr O'Connor'll want to get acquainted with our set-up, that's all,' he said, finding himself cast in the unusual role of mollifier. 'It's no secret that some of the other companies beneath the Betancourts' umbrella are in need of attention, but not us. We may be comparatively small, but we're one of the star performers. He won't intend making changes here.'

Her green eyes glittered. 'He'd better not!'

'Is there something wrong with your house?' Kevin enquired, when the impassioned rearrangement of her desk continued. He was the worrier, the clown who lay awake at nights; while Gabrielle sailed along full of unburstable confidence. Throughout their association he had never known a problem to faze her. She thrived on challenges, on stress. He could think of no current business stresses, thank goodness, yet over the past few days he had watched her grow increasingly distracted. Agitated, almost. 'I know the surveyor swore the place was sound,' he carried on, 'but the previous owners were amazingly keen to get rid of it and——'

'My house is perfect. The ultimate dream.' The papers were abandoned and her boots retrieved. 'But you're right, I should've activated that alarm.' She rose to her feet. 'I'll go and see to it now.'

'Now?' The turnaround made him blink. 'What about Mr O'Connor?'

'You can deal with him.'

His face fell. 'Me?'

'We are in partnership,' she reminded him, collecting a tailored black-and-white hound's-tooth-check coat from the stand.

'But when people think of Anniversaries they think of Gabrielle Peters, and it's Gabrielle Peters he'll expect to meet. The shops are your brainchild. You're the one who found the gap in the market, and filled it,' Kevin said, with a plaintive grin of appeal. 'You're the one who has stock details at her fingertips. 'You're the one——'

'Whose idea of bookkeeping is something done on the backs of old envelopes,' she interrupted. 'Wonder Boy'll want to see figures, which means he'll want to see——' a black fedora was plonked on her head and her bag hooked over one shoulder '—you.'

Deserting Kevin was a lousy trick, Gabrielle acknowledged as she threw 'I'll be back this afternoon' at Tracy, her secretary, in the outer office, and sped on to the corridor. He might be able to recite the balance sheet backwards, sideways, upside-down, but his knowledge of the essential business was patchy—and she doubted their visitor would be satisfied with anything less than a fully painted picture. A pang of remorse hit her. She was wrong to exit like this. She did not *want* to exit, but . . . Ever since a main board *putsch* had ousted the former chief executive and replaced him with a younger, smarter, more hard-hitting individual—a 'saviour' had been implied—she had known it was her destiny to face up to Saul O'Connor some time. Yet she had not imagined it would be so soon.

Soon? jeered a voice in her head; even if the business papers have kept you more or less *au fait* with his activities, it is almost eight years since you last saw the man—and eight years is a long time. Reaching the bank of lifts, Gabrielle pressed the call button. Eight years ago she had been naïve, impressionable, a froth-headed child. Now she was mature, shrewd and acclaimed as runner-up in the Businesswoman of the Year awards! So why the panic?

She nodded hello to a passing youth from the cashier's department, then straightened. That Saul O'Connor should make a comeback into her life was a very strange twist of fate, but falling apart like this was ridiculous. An about-turn was performed. She would go back to her office—her stylish, hi-tech metallic grey and white office—and when he arrived she would greet him with a cool aplomb which made it plain that, whatever had happened in the past, it was no longer of consequence. None. He would understand all wounds had healed, all memories had faded. That she did not give a damn! A step in return had been taken when abruptly an indication light shone, a bell pinged and doors slid aside. Before she could stop herself, Gabrielle was inside the empty lift and pushing the lozenge marked for the lobby.

She could see him another time. Better if she did, she rationalised hurriedly. This afternoon she would prepare a detailed account of Anniversaries' rise and rise, and have Tracy print it out on her word processor. A written screed would be far more comprehensive than any verbal recital. Then tomorrow she would telephone, apologise for not being available and suggest an alternative arrangement. Gabrielle pulled on black gloves, pushing the leather down between her fingers. The notion of *her* fixing a meeting was comforting because, somehow, it transferred the whip hand.

At twenty-eight, Saul O'Connor had been lean, well-muscled and far prettier than any man had a right to be, she thought as the lift descended—what did he look like now? The business pages carried few photographs, and it was ages since she had seen one, but the mid-thirties were notorious for the onset of middle-age spread. Kevin, for example, had gained several unflattering pounds lately, and he was barely a year past the big three-O. How had the passage of time dealt with his idol? she wondered. Tennis *aficionado* or not, could he have thickened around the waist? Did he now toddle behind a pot belly? Maybe his hair had begun to thin? Gabrielle smiled. Her figure was in excellent shape and her coppery hair remained as lush and bouncy as ever, but—the smile edged towards a smirk—the more she thought about it, the more likely it seemed that the ghost from her past could well have altered beyond all recognition. Perhaps, poor soul, he would be revealed as portly, balding, *ordinary*. There would be poetic justice in that!

It was not so. As the lift came to rest and she stepped out into the high chandeliered lobby, a fast-striding man in a flapping trenchcoat collided with her.

'Sorry,' he said, and would have continued inside to take her place if she, too, had gone on her way.

Instead an abrupt lack of oxygen, a paralysis of the knees, rooted her to the spot. The only part of

Gabrielle which moved was her heart, and that had begun beating at a mile a minute. Gazing up from beneath the brim of her hat, she saw that the pretty boy had vanished and what Saul O'Connor looked like now was a man. A man who worked hard and played hard. His face had thinned, etching his features more keenly and leaving his jaw squarer and blunter than she remembered, yet the Celtic contrast of pale blue eyes and peat-dark hair packed the same visual punch. A punch made all the more dramatic by a maple-syrup tan. A punch which must still have women toppling over in droves. So far as she could tell, his six feet three inches remained—exasperatingly—the ideal male shape of broad shoulders, flat stomach, slim hips and long legs. As for his hair which he now wore overlong, it persisted in being thick and glossy.

'Anything the matter?' he enquired, when she continued to stand there. Bending to peer beneath her black fedora, he gave a startled exclamation of recognition. 'Gabby! My, you've changed!'

Indignation jerked her back to life. 'How?' she demanded.

As his eyes swept from the top of her hat to her Italian-leather-clad feet, his mouth tweaked. 'I'd heard "Superwoman" was your middle name these days, but no one told me you'd become so . . . classy.'

In the belief that her personal appearance ought to reflect her professionalism, over the years Gabrielle had consciously revamped herself. She had been delighted with the newly minted version, but now her hackles rose. Superficially he appeared to be paying a compliment, yet something in the gleam of his eyes said he found the difference in her amusing. Saul O'Connor always had possessed an unreliable sense of humour, she thought scathingly.

'Classy?' she repeated, in a dental-drill voice.

'Don't get me wrong. You look terrific. A lesson in designer-desirability.' The tweak became a full-blown grin. 'But not at all like the Gabby I knew.'

'People call me Gabrielle now,' she informed him.

'Do they?' A brow arched. 'The Gabby I remember used to slop around in blue jeans, pink day-glo leg-warmers and baggy sweaters. And wear a pair of old thermal pyjamas in bed—for the two seconds before I took them off.'

To her fury she felt a blush, as hot as a heat rash, spread all over her body. Why did he have to say that? They were strangers now, mere acquaintances. He had no right to bowl in and be so cavalier! It was not fair. It was impolite. It was a darn sight too *familiar*!

'You'll have to excuse me,' Gabrielle said, tugging her hat lower over her eyes, 'but I wasn't aware you were coming until a few minutes ago and—and I have an emergency at home.' The distant glass doors received a pointed, and somewhat desperate, look. 'Kevin will provide all the information you need. That's Kevin Holland, my partner. When I first started in business, the bank manager recommended him as a reliable person to manage my books, and we've been together ever since. In the early days he was a whiz at juggling the cash around, and now he keeps me on the financial straight and narrow. Tells me what I can and can't do. Or tries. Sometimes he's overcautious, but——' Aware of rattling away like a Gatling gun, she stopped. When she was nervous she had a tendency to talk too much. 'Kevin's a good influence,' she completed abruptly.

Saul brushed flakes of wet snow out of his hair. 'What emergency?'

For a split second, her mind was a blank. 'Oh, the burglar alarm. It's a de-luxe job. You can isolate various parts of the house, like the roof, and keep them guarded while you're in residence. However——' hearing herself gabbling again, Gabrielle wound down '—I forgot to actuate it.'

'You're cancelling our appointment in order to switch on a bell?' he said, disbelief rife.

'It's important.' Her chin lifted. 'And we didn't have an appointment. If you recall, you just left a message.'

'I'm supposed to apply for an audience in writing? You would've preferred me to come on bended knee, is that it? Send one of your minions to fix the alarm,' Saul ordered.

'But——'

'Never heard of the subtle art of delegation?'

'Of course.' Gabrielle twisted the question around to suit herself. 'Which is why I've arranged for Kevin to pass on——'

'I came here this morning to discuss your

company with you.'

'Look——'

'*You*! All I'm asking for is a little co-operation, but——' the blue of his eyes darkened ominously '—if you force me to pull rank, I shall have no hesitation in doing so.'

'In that case, I won't bother about the alarm,' she declared.

'You'll just sue me if someone breaks in and swipes your every last teaspoon,' Saul murmured, as she marched back into the lift.

Gabrielle punched the button. 'What made you decide to come back to the UK?' she demanded, when he joined her. 'From all accounts, Betancourts' package means you'll never go short of oysters or champagne . . .'

'As usual, the Press exaggerated everything: the golden hello, my salary, the various performance bonuses,' he cut in, 'but money is not my prime motive. What interests me is . . .' he hesitated, shooting her a quick glance '. . . the challenge, the learning opportunities, the chance I'm being given to widen my scope.'

'Your take-home pay is still prodigious,' she said, deciding to attack where he defended.

Yet he had translated her criticism wrongly. The quarrel was not with how much he earned, but that he now headed the conglomerate which included her company. The situation might be happenstance—far from Saul zeroing in on Anniversaries with the sole intent of becoming her boss, Betancourts' board had sought *him*—yet it still made her seethe.

'When it's a case of "if at first you don't succeed, you're fired", it has to be,' he insisted. 'If I don't turn Betancourts around, and fast, I'll be out on the seat of my pants like the last guy. And that could be all it takes to bring my career to an end. The commercial world doesn't like losers.'

'Surely one failure wouldn't be fatal? After all, you'd still have Sir Jeffrey around,' Gabrielle said pertly, then continued, 'There must have been jobs offering challenge and learning-opportunities in the States.'

Saul pushed back the tousled dark hair which fell over his eyes. 'There were, but——' the lift halted, the doors opening to allow a couple of office girls on board '—but I figured it was time I returned to my roots,' he completed.

Gabrielle attached her eyes to the indicator lights. If he had returned to his roots, so she, on her part, had resurrected feelings she had believed were long dead and buried. Whatever had happened to cool aplomb? she wondered, as the newcomers began a giggly conversation. She watched the numbers increase—eleven, twelve, fourteen. Her aim had been not to show *any* reaction, yet instead she had embarked on an orgy of obstruction and backbiting. A few floors later the lift stopped, and the girls departed. The last few minutes must be obliterated, she decided, as their journey resumed. They would start again. It was the only way.

Gabrielle thrust out a hostess hand. 'I'd like to welcome you to the headquarters of

Anniversaries.'

If Saul was surprised by her change in attitude he gave no sign, but accepted the greeting as formally as it had been given. He glanced down at the briefcase he carried.

'Reading about your achievements in the board minutes was like reading a manual on "How to be a Success in Business".'

'I've been very lucky.'

'But the harder you worked, the luckier you got?'

She granted him a small smile. 'I suppose so, though my staff deserve much of the credit.'

'Most of your employees are female,' he observed, as they reached their destination, 'and the majority work on a part-time basis?'

'The shops are open until mid-evening, so we operate shifts,' Gabrielle explained, recognising that he had already done some of his homework. 'Suppose I gather the office staff together and you can meet them?' she suggested, when coats had been shed and they sat facing each other across her desk.

Some kind of conciliatory gesture would not go amiss, and with her nerves settling down—even though it was only into a facsimile of their usual order—she was able to be generous.

'Another day. Mind if I smoke?' Saul enquired, and when she shook her head he slid a hand inside the jacket of his perfectly cut, dark grey flannel suit and drew out a slim silver case. 'My primary objective this morning is to hear your view on where Anniversaries is going,' he explained, lighting a cigar.

'Well, in the short term we're opening shops outside London. Five are planned for late summer and another four before Christmas. Plus a new warehouse complex is scheduled.' She tilted a quizzical head. 'But you must know that already.'

'I do. I'm also aware that no site has actually been acquired. That to date nothing has been signed. That no binding commitments have been made.'

'Well . . . no,' Gabrielle agreed, chary all of a sudden. 'However, negotiations are in the final stages,' she emphasised brightly.

'I've told Betancourts' property department to go no further.'

She stared at him aghast. 'I beg your pardon?'

'I've given instructions for everything to be put on condition amber.' Saul drew at his cigar. 'For the moment.'

'Condition amber?' She straightened the cropped jacket of her black wool suit. Worn with a strict white blouse, the outfit was what fashion writers described as radical chic. 'Why?' she demanded.

'Because I need to evaluate whether or not expansion along those lines is right for Anniversaries.'

Gabrielle surveyed him through a mist of blue-grey smoke. The previous chief executive had been amenable to anything and everything where Anniversaries was concerned—a regular pussycat.

But the decisive tone and authoritative air marked his replacement down as a tiger. And, as everyone knew, tigers pounced, ripped, mauled!

'But I've already been given the go-ahead,' she protested. The inter-office phone buzzed. 'Yes?' she demanded, snapping down the switch.

'Tracy tells me you and Mr O'Connor are in conference, and I wondered whether there's anything you need from me,' Kevin's disembodied voice asked merrily.

She flung her visitor an enquiring look, but he shook his head.

'Not just now, thanks,' she said, thinking that this was not a conference, it was Saul unsheathing his claws—or trying to. 'Why don't you want me to open more branches?' she blitzed, the moment the line had cleared.

'I didn't say that,' he replied, as she stalked round to confront him. 'All I said, Gabby, was——'

'Gabrielle!'

'—I need time to decide, *Peters*.'

'Peters?' she repeated, momentarily knocked off course.

'You won't agree to Gabby and I'm sure as hell not calling you Gabrielle, so——' He shrugged.

'Opening more branches *has* been decided!' she declared. Compared to the current issue, how he addressed her was a minor matter, something she would deal with later.

Saul hooked an arm over the back of his chair and gazed angelically up. 'I'm sorry if you regard this as an invasion of your territory, but Betancourts' ownership of two-thirds of Anniversaries' voting-rights does give me some clout.' He located an ashtray from the mêlée on her desk. 'Do you have agreement to the purchase of the properties in writing?' he enquired, knocking ash from his cigar.

Her eyes shot emerald daggers. He already knew the answer to that!

'I wasn't aware it was necessary. In the past——'

'The previous guy didn't operate the way I operate,' Saul put in.

'Obviously not!'

He sighed. 'You must see it's impossible for me to rubber-stamp his ideas until I'm convinced they're worth while.'

'Opening up more shops was *my* idea,' Gabrielle declared heatedly, 'and it *is* worth while. Anniversaries occupies an extremely profitable niche in the anniversary, birthday and Christmas-gift market. As it says in our literature, we take the tussle out of present-buying and make it fun. OK, launching any new outlet contains an element of risk, but as the shops are proven winners, in this case it's minuscule! Now, if you intend to argue that London customers are a different breed from those elsewhere, I do not agree,' she pronounced, gathering speed. 'A store which is bright, friendly, inspirational, will be a success anywhere. People enjoy walking into Anniversaries here and they'll enjoy walking into Anniversaries in Birmingham, in Manchester, in——'

'Could I put a foot up on the soapbox,' Saul interrupted, 'and say that while I'm all for things getting better, I'd query whether it necessarily equates with bigger? There's a lot in favour of being a David among the Goliaths, but being excellent. If your short-term intention's to damn near double the number of outlets in less than a year,' he went on, 'then I can only assume your medium and long-term goals are more and even more shops?'

Her spine stiffened. 'Yes.'

'Until there's an Anniversaries around every street corner?'

'More or less.'

'This projected development is the result of an assessment of trends? Of you working out how many outlets the market should be able to support? You've evolved a conscious strategy which stipulates shops opening at certain times and in certain places?'

In all honesty Gabrielle's flair was for creative day-by-day advancement, not detailed forward planning, but she refused to confess to blurred vision.

'Everything's been considered. And once a nationwide chain's established we shall open branches overseas,' she announced grandly.

'You intend to function on the global scene,' Saul mused. 'Isn't that rather ambitious?'

'Not in the least.'

Gravely he stubbed out his cigar, then rose to prowl across the room. For a minute or two he gazed at the falling snow. 'What makes you so keen to enlarge your empire?' he enquired eventually.

Gabrielle twirled in her swivel-chair to stare. What kind of a question was that?

'I consider growth to be the natural progression.' She did not add 'Dumbo', but it was implied.

'Is it the financial rewards which appeal?' asked Saul, sagging a shoulder against the window. 'You long for a seven-figure bank account?'

'No, the money's a bi-product,' she began in protest.

'You get a kick out of the power?'

'Not at all. I——'

'You crave the glory?' Gabrielle shook her head. 'Then what's in expansion for you personally?'

Her brow furrowed. She had never stopped to define whys and wherefores, and now she was mystified. Her original ambition had, she supposed, been inspired by the need to establish her own identity and to show everyone, including herself, that she could succeed doing her own thing in her own way. This had been amply demonstrated long ago, so why did she continue to stumble home hollow with exhaustion? Gabrielle wondered. What kept her pacing the treadmill? Why did she intend to spend the future running and running and running?

'My first shop was a cubicle on the Strand,' she began, tacking together a few thoughts. 'At the start I couldn't open in the mornings because I needed to go office temping in order to finance it. Then someone told me about a loan-guarantee scheme, and Kevin and I joined forces, and in two years we shot from nowhere to become——' Gabrielle lost patience. 'I've devoted over seven years to Anniversaries, most of my adult life, and it means everything to me. When you've watched something grow from a few rackety shelves to a popular chain of stores—when *you've* made it grow—it becomes a part of you. Anniversaries is my pride and joy. Anniversaries is——'

'Your baby,' Saul rasped.

The world seemed to judder. Tilt. Stop. Tense as a stretched catapult, she looked at him, and for an endless moment his blue eyes burned into hers, then he was striding back to extract a file from his briefcase.

'You focus on quality goods, yet do a brisk trade in kitsch,' he said, leafing through what she recognised as stock inventories. 'Presumably that coaxes a wider range of customers into the shops?'

Gabrielle swallowed, and eased off a notch. 'Um, yes.'

The next half-hour was spent answering questions which came thick and fast. The ink might barely be dry on her visitor's contract, but what one journalist had called his 'Rolls-Royce business brain' was already functioning in top gear.

'I'd like to take a look around one of your stores,' Saul said, when the inquisition was over.

'Give me date and time, and I'll arrange for someone to act as tour guide,' she offered.

'No,' he said, 'I need you.'

Gabrielle winced. The phrase was just a figure of speech, yet, as his previous comment had evoked disturbing memories, so the three short words prompted thoughts of being held in his arms, of urgent whispers, of his naked body hard against hers.

'Me?' she bleated. 'Why me?'

'Because you know more about the business than anyone else.'

She shook a fevered head. 'I assure you, any of the manageresses can . . .'

Her protest petered out as long-fingered hands curled around the edge of the desk and he leant towards her.

'I'm not asking you to donate a kidney, dammit!' Saul grated, and she heard real anger in his voice.

Surprised, Gabrielle stared at him. Eight years ago, one of the qualities which had—initially—delighted her had been his easy control. Lesser mortals might grow tense, or shout, or head-bang in fury, yet he had remained forever good-humoured, forever in charge of himself and his surroundings. As he had grown older, Saul, it was becoming apparent, had shed some of his equanimity—but then, she reflected, he could not have achieved his track record for pruning companies, steamrollering through decisions, wrestling with unions, without the deployment of large amounts of grit.

'I'll be pleased to show you around,' Gabrielle

assured him primly.

'Many thanks.' His bow was one hundred per cent sarcasm. 'I'm tied up for the next couple of weeks, so suppose we meet at the Kensington branch, say nine a.m. a fortnight on Thursday?'

'I'll be there.'

Saul walked to the door, where he paused and turned. 'You'd better be,' he said.

CHAPTER TWO

WITH one blast the wind dismantled Gabrielle's topknot, sending copper-gold strands tumbling down her shoulders and plastering them across her face. So much for the *soignée* look! Gabrielle thought, hauling handfuls of hair from her eyes. The snow, now reduced to dirty white heaps in the gutters, had been succeeded by a force-ten Siberian gale, and fearful of seeing her hat disappear across the rooftops she had opted to go bareheaded. Gabrielle shivered. It had been a dismal idea. Only a few steps had been taken from the mews on to the High Street, yet already her ears were frozen, and with her hair blowing around like demented seaweed she must resemble the Wild Woman from the West.

'Cold enough for you, darlin'?' someone asked.

'Just about,' she grinned, refixing the silver and tortoiseshell comb as best she could.

Her questioner was the man who sold fruit and vegetables from a barrow on the corner. She had been his customer for less than a month, yet as she had paused to choose from among the oranges, bananas, the polished red apples—lunch was invariably munched on the run—a camaraderie had been established. For her part, she wanted to integrate into the neighbourhood. For him, he always enjoyed chatting up the girls. And this little charmer was something special. On the surface she seemed a slick, modern miss capable of saying a darn sight more than 'boo' to a goose, yet in the depths of those huge green eyes lurked a vulnerability which tugged at his heartstrings.

'Want someone to cuddle up to?' he enquired, wiggling bushy grey eyebrows.

Her dimples bewitched him. 'No, thanks.'

'And here was I, all set to ask the missus if she'd loan me out for the night!' he exclaimed, voicing extravagant regrets.

With a laugh Gabrielle said goodbye, but as she twisted her scarf more snugly around her neck and joined the people hurrying along the pavement her amusement faded. Ever since Saul's visit a question had been darting in and out of her mind like a pesky mouse and, yet again, it winked its beady eye. Precisely why had he insisted on putting the purchase of the new Anniversaries premises on ice?

When appraised of the situation, Kevin had been unconcerned.

'You can't expect the guy to agree to something he hasn't had time to consider properly,' her partner had protested. 'But he's a quick thinker, so any delay's bound to be minimal. This is a hiccup, that's all.'

Gabrielle wished she could be so sanguine, but to her the hold-off smacked of something . . . sinister. For one thing, if Saul equated with Einstein on wheels, why hadn't he recognised the potential of

her plans and given his straightforward
agreement? Opening more Anniversaries branches
involved no anguished cogitations, no great
debate. For another, she fretted, Kevin did not
know the man as she did. He had no idea how
clever Saul O'Connor was at creating misleading
impressions. He had no inkling how machiavellian
he could be.

The staccato stomp of her heels along the
pavement quickened. It was always possible Saul
had thrown a spanner in the works deliberately to
annoy her. Aware of her impetuous, do-it-now
nature, it could appeal to his oddball sense of
humour to make her sweat. *Gabby* was tearing her
hair. *Gabby* was gnawing on her knuckles. Funny,
ha ha! Or maybe holding matters in abeyance was
him taking his revenge for her walking out so many
years ago? Even though he would have been
delighted to find her gone, it must have been a
blow to his ego that he had not dismissed her
himself. Perhaps he was involved in a text-book
exercise of macho posturing? she mused, as she
joined the crowd waiting at the pedestrian crossing.
Something along the lines of 'I'm in charge. I call
the shots, not you.' She tapped an irritated foot. If
delay was the way Saul intended to play things, so
be it. But one thing was certain—she refused to
give him the satisfaction of asking about the new
shops again. And when he raised the subject, she
would be imperially offhand.

Gabrielle checked her watch. Five minutes past
nine. Damn! She was late for their meeting, which

meant she, the woman who specialised in punctuality as an example to her staff, had been late twice recently. And today she had only herself to blame. A month ago moving from rented flat to mews house had coincided with a battery of meetings, leaving her possessions to be deposited willy-nilly around the rooms. Weekends had been designated as sort-out times, but business—in the form of an unexpected visit from an overseas supplier, a crisis over publicity, the installation of a new manageress—had successively encroached, so chaos still prevailed. This morning the Kensington branch's proximity had made travelling to the office only to return a short time later pointless and, gifted with a free hour, she had embarked on a spurt of intensive cleaning. The plan had been to devote sixty wondrous minutes to the kitchen, then enjoy a leisurely bath before she dressed and sallied forth. Some hopes! The not unknown sin of attempting to squeeze too much into too short a time had been committed, leaving her to hurtle through wash, brush and change at the speed of sound.

Gabrielle willed either the light to change or the traffic to thin. Neither obliged. She looked at her watch again. If nothing else, this morning had taught her one thing—getting her home shipshape and orderly would require far longer than a weekend. She reached a decision. Come Monday, she would take a week off work. The break would be her first in more than a year and anything but a holiday, yet it would make a change. She smiled.

The prospect of seven days of washing down paintwork, lining drawers, placing her belongings on shelves, seemed oddly appealing.

At last the green man shone, and Gabrielle dashed across the road. Usually the people who thronged Kensington High Street fascinated her, but this morning she did not notice the Nigerian in his flowing embroidered robes, a clutch of county matrons in their furs and pearls, the cockerel-headed punks heading for the leather and chain delights of the indoor market. Speed was all. If only she had not become so engrossed in wire-woolling the cooker, she grumbled, as she powered past the elegant department stores and kinky-boo boutiques. If only she could have been on time. The design had been to knock Saul dead with her efficiency, but this tardy start awarded no Brownie points. In the distance the silver-grey and white 'Anniversaries' sign glinted in the winter sunshine, and her stride increased to a jog. A rapid swerve, a few 'excuse me's, a final sprint, and she pushed open the shiny glass door.

The shop was empty. The chief executive had yet to show—alleluia! Pink-faced and breathless, Gabrielle removed her coat and straightened her lavender-blue blouse and matching high-waisted skirt. Her hair had been tidied and her face inspected, before chatter wafting out from the staff-room at the rear penetrated. Given half a chance, Amanda, the jaunty blonde who ran the store, would talk the hind leg off the proverbial donkey, and today her dialogue sounded even more quickfire than usual. Gabrielle frowned. Whatever the topic, the manageress's conversation was inappropriate. A generous three minutes had gone by since her entrance, and it was high time either Amanda or her assistant came out to greet her. Good customer relations were the cornerstone of any successful retailing business, she thought impatiently, and for all they knew she could be someone needing advice, someone wishing to make a purchase, someone who, if she was not served immediately, would walk out never to return.

Glancing right and left, Gabrielle went down the shop. The grey-and-white colour scheme provided a perfect backdrop for Anniversaries' eclectic mix of merchandise, and as usual the colourful displays brought a warm glow—though today a brief one. Amanda was *still* talking, *still* closeted out of sight, *still* shunning her duties.

'And next there was the matter of his shirts. I don't mind ironing them, what I do mind is him shoving half a dozen at me, then saying he had to meet someone,' she heard the blonde complain. 'When Mike returned, I told him it wasn't good enough, but he accused me of nagging. Now I don't know what to do. What do you think?'

In unison, Gabrielle's momentum and irritation increased. For months the manageress had been beset with boyfriend trouble, but this was neither the time nor the place for airing the current calamity. And her second-in-command should have known better than to desert the shop to listen. Marching like a drill sergeant, Gabrielle wheeled through the arch.

'Please could you——?'

She ground to abrupt attention. Leaning forward in a chair, with hands loosely clasped between his knees, was Saul. His appearance—navy pin-striped suit, immaculate white shirt, dark silk tie—was business tycoon personified, yet no business had been done. On the contrary, the empty coffee mug beside him, plus his at-home ease, indicated he had been a participating audience for quite a while. Gabrielle's mouth pinched. It was galling enough to find that, far from being late, he had firmly established himself in *her* shop with *her* staff, but what chafed most was the moonstruck way the manageress gazed at him. Eyes round, glossy red mouth parted in query, Amanda waited hungrily for his advice—and looked ready to gulp down whatever pearls of wisdom he might deign to toss.

'I'd be obliged if you'd cut out the chat,' Gabrielle barked, as irritation condensed into anger. Her green eyes strafed first the manageress and then the motherly, grey-haired woman who acted as deputy. 'Somebody should be in the shop at all times; that *is* what you're paid for.'

In a haste of dismay and embarrassment, the two women leapt to their feet.

'I'm sorry,' Amanda gabbled.

'Me, too,' apologised her assistant.

'So you should be. There's no room for

passengers here!'

'It's my fault,' Amanda hurried on. 'I became so involved talking about Mike that I forgot——'

'You should *not* forget. And as far as that boyfriend of yours is concerned, if you had any sense you'd get rid of him.'

The blonde's jaw dropped. 'What?'

'He's had you waiting on him hand and foot from Day One, though much of it's your own fault because you've placed yourself in the subordinate role,' Gabrielle bit out.

'Sub—subordinate?'

'Are all his limbs attached?'

'Er—yes.'

'Then tell him to iron his own damn shirts. Now, off you go, and don't leave the shop unoccupied again—ever!'

'Er—no,' Amanda said, looking dazed.

A thumb was jerked. 'Now!'

Babbling apologies, the manageress scuttled out with the older woman close behind her.

'And a very good morning to you, too, Peters,' Saul said, rising from his chair. His mouth curved. 'Remind me again, when was it you graduated from charm school?'

'The same year you gained your qualification as agony aunt,' she retorted. If he imagined he could reduce the situation to a joke, he had miscalculated. It was no laughing matter. She was not amused by his use of her surname, either. 'I understood your purpose today was to learn more about the business, not aid and abet my staff in the neglect of their duties,' Gabrielle snapped. 'Having received a cup of coffee, anyone else would've had the good grace to stand to one side and allow them to get on with their work, but did you? Oh, no!'

'Hey, when I arrived I found Amanda tense and anxious,' he protested. 'It was barely nine and there were no customers, so when she started to air her problems I listened—though I had no idea she would talk for so long.' Saul shone a soothing smile. 'I don't expect you to perform a cartwheel of joy, but don't you think that in shouting like that you were being a little bit over-zealous? At one point I was afraid the poor girl might need to be carried out on a stretcher.'

Gabrielle glared. 'I did not shout.'

'No? Well, you certainly had quite an edge there. Ever read the book about how Al Capone got started?' he continued ingenuously. 'You should. It shows how, if you're not careful, one thing can lead to another, and before you know it——'

'To hell with Al Capone!'

He raised two innocent hands. 'Just trying to lighten the mood here. Y'know,' Saul continued, with a grin, 'all this rampaging fury of yours is enough to set a bishop's trousers on fire.'

Whenever she had lost her temper in the past he had found her sexy—not a result she had ever intended or relished—and belatedly she noticed his fascination with the rise and fall of her breasts beneath the lavender-blue silk. Gabrielle's hands tightened into fists.

'And to hell with——'

'Me?' Saul completed, when she broke off to tilt her head. In the shop, the twang of transatlantic accents announced that customers had arrived to make the first purchases of the day. 'Sorry to disappoint you, but I'm not extinguished that easily.' A snow-white cuff was realigned. 'Shall we make a start? I notice that, as far as possible, you separate your stock into gifts for men and gifts for women.'

This reversal to business took her by surprise, and Gabrielle needed to make a severe mental effort in order to follow his lead.

'We do,' she agreed. 'And because we've discovered that the amount people have to spend is often the criterion, everything is then separated into easily identifiable price ranges.'

'Which go from?'

'I'll show you.'

As they circuited the shop, self-recrimination quickly arrived. Amanda had deserved some form of reprimand but, Gabrielle admitted with regret, she should never have ranted and raved. Good staff were both her allies and her ambassadors, yet now the manageress might say 'no, thanks' to friendship and keep her distance. As for castigating Betancourts' chief executive—like it or not, he was an on-going entity with a direct influence on her company, and common sense insisted she would be unwise to antagonise him too much. She sighed. Her handling of the last few minutes had been abysmal, but unfortunately whenever Saul was around she seemed incapable of handling anything. Her usual composure deserted her, and instead she functioned on pure, reckless and unstoppable emotion.

Gabrielle enumerated stock, opened boxes, explained which lines sold best and when. Details of how displays and advertising matched Christmas, St Valentine's Day, and other special events on the calendar were given, plus a hundred and one other facts.

'Anything else you'd like to know?' she asked, reaching the end of almost an hour's non-stop spiel.

Saul's lips moved into a droll curve. 'I figure you've just about covered the lot.'

Their tour had finished beside the glass door, and Gabrielle held out a hand. 'Then if that's it, I'll say goodbye. I have a busy day ahead, and I know you must have too.' Her handshake was firm, brief and dismissive. 'If you should think of something I've forgotten, I'll be pleased to be of service,' she assured him, and headed off for the store-room.

She was half-way down the shop when Amanda waylaid her.

'Excuse me, but last week I read an article about fob watches being the latest "in" male accessory, and yesterday we had two enquiries. I wondered if we ought to be selling them?'

'Could be popular,' Gabrielle agreed. The assistant was attending to the current customers, so she gestured for the blonde to accompany her through the arch. 'I shouldn't have snapped at you earlier,' she said, with an apologetic smile. 'Please will you forgive me?'

Amanda grinned. 'Yes, but you were right—about how I should've been watching the shop, and about Mike. Much as I love him, I have to confess he's a member of the women-as-chattels brigade.' She wrinkled her nose. 'I've been moaning about the way he treats me for ages, but I suspect the time has come for me to act.'

'Act? How?' Gabrielle asked, perturbed all of a sudden. 'For heaven's sake, don't finish with him unless you're positive it's what you want. Nothing and nobody is perfect, and sometimes you have to compromise. Sometimes a person's good points enable you to overlook the bad. Sometimes you have to accept that people are different, and what may seem a major fault to you is just——' The waterfall of words dried up. A spirited advocate of female independence, she was astonished to hear herself fudging the issue and backtracking. 'I'll look into fob watches and keep you informed,' she promised lamely.

Amanda giggled. 'I had such a shock when Mr O'Connor walked in. You see, there was a picture of him in the *Mail* this morning with Dana Kelham.'

She reached for her coat. 'Who?'

'That television reporter. The one with the slinky figure and masses of black hair who does those investigative programmes. Anyhow, it seemed like one minute I was looking at Mr

O'Connor over my cornflakes, and the next we came face to face.'

'*Quelle horreur,*' Gabrielle could not resist saying, but the blonde was immune.

'He's so approachable and so attractive. And that grin—ooh!' Amanda shivered with delight. 'It puts every other grin I've ever seen right in the shade. He and Dana were photographed at some expensive restaurant. "Heads down and deep in conversation," the caption said. Do you think they're going steady?'

'I've no idea.' Gabrielle tossed her white mohair scarf over one shoulder. ''Bye.'

Maybe Saul had only been back in the country a short time, but that would not prevent him from being involved in a torrid affair, she thought as she walked down the shop. When it came to persuading women to go to bed with him, he was no slouch. Though precious little persuasion had been required in her case. As her mind catapulted back, she squirmed. She had been so willing. So ripe. So eager. All he had needed to do was smile and caress her lips with his finger and . . . A group of French students were admiring paperweights on a central gondola, and as she completed the circumnavigation her step faltered. She had assumed Betancourts' chief executive had left, but he was waiting beside the door, one hand in a trouser pocket. Gabrielle stared in dismay. To see him in print then in person might have surprised Amanda, but she found this juxtaposition of lover in her head with Saul, the physical man, standing before her, utterly disconcerting.

'Yes?' she demanded, in a gaspy squeak.

He smiled. 'I take it you're going to your office, and as I'm heading in roughly the same direction I thought we could go together.' He raised a farewell hand to Amanda and her sidekick, and ushered her outside. 'My car's parked across the road.'

'Thanks, but I wouldn't want to take you out of your way,' Gabrielle said quickly. 'And the Tube goes almost door to door.'

'Unless it's been re-sited during my absence, the Underground's a good half-mile from here, while my transport happens to be within stone-throwing distance,' Saul replied, standing firm.

'It's kind of you to offer——' her smile was of the instant-whip variety '—but I really think it'd be easier if——'

'You specialise in braving sub-arctic conditions?' he demanded, as the wind yanked at his tie and flattened his hair back from his brow.

'No, but——'

'Then stop giving me the cold shoulder.' Flint had entered Saul's voice and his blue eyes. 'The past is gone, Gabby. Gone!'

'I beg your pardon?' she said, startled.

'Forget it.' His tone eased. 'I just thought travelling together would give us a chance to talk.'

Talk? Her business antennae shot up. When they had first met they had talked about everything under the moon, the stars and the sun, but now the only subject the two of them could possibly discuss was Anniversaries. Had his 'condition amber' changed to 'condition green'? she wondered. Excitement bubbled. After more than two weeks on tenterhooks, if he had agreed that everything could proceed, she needed to know today.

Gabrielle gave the most casual shrug she could muster.

'Lead on.'

His car, a wine-red 5-series BMW, had been lodged in an underground car park, and a few minutes later they were heading up the ramp and out into the daylight.

'How many buyers do you have?' Saul enquired, as he swung the saloon on to the narrow side street.

'I don't. The purchasing department deals with the paperwork, import licences, shipping and so on, but I choose the goods myself.'

She received a narrow-eyed glance. 'You select every item single-handed?'

Gabrielle nodded. 'Once a year I go on what Kevin calls my "grand tour" and visit suppliers in this country, plus I scour Europe, America and Asia in the hope of finding something different. I'm away a full six weeks.'

'No one else buys *anything*?' Saul demanded.

'Why should they? It's my taste, my choices, which have made Anniversaries the shops they are.'

'Agreed, but——' He shook his head in wry amazement. 'I overheard Amanda suggest the watches. You took note of that.'

'I'm always open to ideas.'

'Then you admit other people can have good ones?'

'Naturally. I would never claim to know it all.'

'If the number of shops doubles or even trebles, what happens then?' asked Saul. 'Do you still plan to purchase the entire stock?'

'Yes.'

'And keep a watching brief over every branch?'

'It's the way I work.'

His brows drew together. 'According to Amanda, you're already on the go from eight a.m. until near enough midnight, so——'

'You've been discussing me with my employees?' Gabrielle demanded astringently.

'Data-gathering is one of the ways in which *I* work,' he replied, unrepentant. 'So—given you must sleep some time, how can you increase your workload?'

She scowled. 'I'll manage,' she assured him.

'At what cost?'

'Cost? Why should there be a cost. I'm young. I'm healthy. I'm forever stimulated by what I do.'

'There is such a thing as burn-out.'

'And you think I ought to have more knock-off ability—well, sorry, I don't!'

Saul cast her a look. 'You did once. Once you had the mix of work and play just right.'

She greeted his reminder with a flashbulb smile. 'Everyone's entitled to their opinions.'

'Public success doesn't mean a thing if your private life's a shambles,' he said quietly. 'Business is not the be-all and—oh, hell!'

Earlier, the traffic had been moving freely, but a turn on to the High Street had slammed them up against a wall of vehicles. Saul nosed the BMW half-way into a gap between two taxis and, after a couple of minutes when everything remained staunchly immobile, sighed and applied the handbrake.

'Did you know that the average speed of vehicles through Central London is eight miles an hour, which isn't much more than it was in the horse-and-cart days a hundred years ago?' Gabrielle enquired sweetly.

She was a victim of the traffic, too, but in the wake of his self-confidence of a moment before Saul's impotence was something to be savoured.

'You always were a fund of useless information,' he muttered, squinting ahead at the cars, lorries and double-decker buses which stretched out along the perimeter of Hyde Park to the horizon. 'Know any short cuts?'

''Fraid not. I'm a newcomer to the district.'

'You've recently become the proud owner of a mews house, I believe.'

'This is more data gathered from my staff?' Gabrielle said, in a sandpapery voice.

'No gathering required. In this instance the information was pressed upon me. Do you live alone? What about a boyfriend, occasional caller, sugar daddy or whatever?' Saul asked, when she nodded.

'Why don't you ask Amanda?' she parried.

'Because she isn't here. Is there a man in your life?' he repeated.

Gabrielle hesitated. She regarded any relationships as *her* affair and no business of his—yet to refuse to answer seemed too much like overkill.

'I'm much too busy for——' she began, with a flippant wave of a hand, but a buzz cut her short.

'Excuse me.' Saul reached down to lift a matt black car-phone. 'Hello? Oh, it's you, Dana.' Having established his caller's identity, he turned away to cradle the handset against his collarbone. 'Yes?'

In the minutes which followed, his watchful huddle and monosyllabic answers made it clear a matter 'just between the two of them' was under discussion. Gabrielle fixed her eyes on the taxi ahead of them. If he did not relish having an audience, neither did she enjoy being forced to play gooseberry to a conversation which reeked of intimacy. Her scarf was loosened and the top button of her coat unfastened. Earlier, she had been on the brink of revealing a dearth of male interest, but now she changed her mind. Call it pride, call it weakness, call it pathetic; but she rebelled against an admission of celibacy when his love-life was so clearly rip-roaring away. She refused to give him the pleasure of classifying her off-duty hours as a shambles.

'Sorry about that,' said Saul, when he finally

unglued the receiver from his ear.

'Never bother,' she trilled. 'You were asking about men. I was involved with someone—heavily involved—but we broke up recently.'

'What was his name?'

Gabrielle looked at him. 'Name?'

Repetition could be useful when you needed time to think, but on this occasion her thought processes remained as stationary as the traffic.

'Maybe he answered to a number?' Saul shifted, resting back against the leather upholstery to gaze at her with steady blue eyes. 'Or maybe "recently" is so long ago, you've forgotten what he was called . . . Or maybe——' the pause tantalised '—he never existed . . .'

The suggestion—so amused, so casual, so accurate—hit like a slap in the face.

'He did, too!' she declared, indignant at his intuition.

'It'd need to be a pretty undemanding kind of guy who'd be satisfied with the few free hours you have on offer. A pretty wimpish guy. A pretty sexless guy.' The corner of his mouth twitched. 'You've not been entertaining a eunuch, have you?'

'That isn't funny!'

Abruptly his amusement faded. 'No, it isn't,' he agreed, 'because I'd bet my life on it you haven't been entertaining anybody recently. What a mix-up in priorities.' Saul sat straighter, closer, making her aware of his size, his masculinity, and how they were encapsulated together. 'When did someone last hold you in his arms, last make love to you? When were you last kissed?' he demanded.

Gabrielle gulped in a breath. 'A couple of months ago.'

'Never,' he murmured and, clasping strong fingers around the back of her head, he drew her to him.

'Saul, please,' she started to protest, but as her lips parted he kissed her. At the pressure of his mouth and the touch of his tongue, the eight years apart vanished. All of a sudden, it was as though they were still together, still lovers, still locked in that sensuous chemistry. For a giddy moment she submitted helplessly to the excitement he provoked, then a nearby horn hooted. Raising both hands, Gabrielle pushed against his chest. 'What—what do you think you're doing?' she demanded shakily.

'Proving a point.' He tucked his tie back into his jacket. 'Y'know, wonderful as those shops of yours may be, they'll never love you back. So if you intend to spend the next ten years with your knees firmly bolted together——'

'You are obnoxious!'

'—it'll be one helluva waste.'

Bereft of an answer, any answer, Gabrielle subjected the taxi to another concentrated scrutiny, until—praise be—the gods provided a diversion.

'You can go now,' she said, and jabbed a finger. 'The traffic's moving, see?'

Sliding into first gear, Saul entered the cut and

thrust of the inner-city scrum. Progress began via a number of stops and starts and gradual acceleration until, in one of those curious circumstances, the bulk of the traffic went left while they swung right. For brief magical minutes he could drive flat out.

'I assume you'll have made your initial assessment of Betancourts' strengths and weaknesses,' Gabrielle remarked. 'Reached any verdicts?'

After the conversation taking such an alarmingly personal turn, she was desperate to return to the world of business—and she hoped to jog his memory about her new shops.

'Some.'

She tried again. 'Kevin says that, according to the grapevine, the printing work's finances aren't too hot.'

'The grapevine's right, they're not. The printing works and the hotel chain are both struggling to survive.'

'The hotels?' she said, her voice rising in surprise.

Saul nodded. 'This is confidential, but for years the minimum has been spent on redecoration and renovation, until it's reached a stage where either they're drastically, and expensively, modernised—or someone puts a bomb under the lot. Personally, I'd go for the second option.'

Gabrielle thought of the grand country mansions which provided hunting, shooting and fishing holidays for the wealthy.

'But the hotels are Betancourts' flagship company,' she protested. 'The directors set tremendous store on their prestige.'

'I'm well aware of that,' he said ruefully. 'My solution would be to split them up and sell them off, but even if I could find takers the board would never agree.'

'So, what do you do? Lop off another part of the conglomerate, and channel the money from that into them?'

Saul sighed. 'I guess. Given a complete overhaul and a new slant, maybe towards the Japanese visitor, the hotels could be profitable.'

As they had neared her office the traffic had increased, and once again they were reduced to 'stop and go'. A wait, a spurt of acceleration, another snail's progress, and eventually the tower block appeared in the distance. Gabrielle was gazing at its soaring height when something she had said to Kevin about Anniversaries' occupying 'prime London locations' came into her mind. She froze. The tower-block accommodation was rented, but her company owned the shops lock, stock and barrel. At the beginning she had opened in areas which had, of necessity, been cheap—until the Yuppies had descended with their Porsches and credit cards and their spend-spend-spending. That the neighbourhoods were destined to become fashionable a few years later, and that property prices should soar in general, had been good fortune, not good management, but it meant that if the cash value of her sites was realised it would amount to millions. Anniversaries' weak point, so Kevin never stopped telling her, was cash flow; and yet they were sitting on a veritable gold-mine.

Gabrielle shot a distrustful glance at the man beside her. Saul's flair for identifying opportunities invisible to the naked eye had generated much respect among City bankers, so what if instead of expansion he happened to be looking in entirely the opposite direction? He had vetoed splitting up and selling off the hotels, but was that what he had in mind for Anniversaries? The idea made a gruesome kind of sense. Dismantle her company, and he would both conserve capital in so much as Betancourts would not be required to finance the new shops, plus release a small fortune with which to renovate the hotels.

Could this be the real reason behind the delay? she wondered, in alarm. Now she recalled Saul's comment on how many of her employees worked short and irregular hours. Unlike full-time staff, the part-timers were not covered by main employment legislation. They could be dismissed without expensive settlements. They would not soak up pension payments. Her head began to thud. Saul had also referred to the conglomerate's holding sixty-six per cent of her shares which meant that, no matter how strongly she might object, he possessed the power to force a sale through. Not only was Anniversaries incontestably disposable, it came gift-wrapped for him!

'The hatchet-man strikes again,' she muttered, recalling a headline from the days when he had been trimming dead wood from Meyers Land.

Saul's jaw tightened. 'Not you, too. OK, the Press goes hysterical, but you must know there's no room for sentiment in business, that sometimes sacrifices need to be made.'

'Like people being thrown out of work?' Gabrielle challenged bitterly. 'Like businesses being decimated and disposed of piecemeal?'

'There are occasions when a minor part must be sacrificed in order to save the major,' he pronounced, with the weary air of having stated his case many times before. 'I agree it isn't fair. I realise it might not appear to make much sense in the short run. I admit people suffer—and I go through hell, too—but often it's the only way.'

He went through hell! Gabrielle's look chopped him into little pieces. Whoever lost out in a deal with Saul O'Connor, she was sure it would never be him.

'In other words, you've made a career out of being ruthless,' she accused, her tone curt with contempt. 'Isn't that a perfect example of fitting the man to the job!'

'Haven't you ever wondered if your view of the past could be faulty?' he demanded, as he pulled the BMW on to the parking-bay outside her offices. 'Hasn't it occurred to you that maybe I was not entirely the big bad wolf?'

'*Never*.' She used the word as incisively as a surgeon would use a scalpel. 'Thank you for the lift,' good manners made her say automatically, as she stepped from the car.

Saul gave a mirthless bark of laughter. 'My pleasure.'

Without a backward glance, Gabrielle strode away. His *pleasure*, she thought, as she rode the lift up to her office, might well be to destroy her future—as he had so effectively wrought havoc with her past! Gabrielle's thoughts drifted back to those days when she had first known Saul . . .

CHAPTER THREE

WHATEVER her misgivings, Gabrielle had been forced to admit that life as a university student promised to be fun and, if the past three days were anything to go by, amazingly hectic, too. Ever since her father had deposited her on the mid-Yorkshire campus, she had been scurrying back and forth—enrolling for classes, tracking down remote and elusive lecture-rooms, meeting her tutors. Even on Saturday the pace did not slacken, for one of the girls who shared the small terraced house had asked if she would go with her to a free-for-all exhibition held by the various sports clubs, hobby associations and special-interest groups.

'The idea is to entice us first-years to join them,' her new-found friend had explained.

When they arrived, the 'enticing' was going full blast. Stalls had been erected around the perimeter of the huge hall, and at each one young men and women were vigorously extolling the virtues of this activity or that. Crowds gathered to listen. Leaflets were read. And, as the two girls pushed their way from one stand to another, they were separated. Marooned among the blue-jeaned masses, Gabrielle made an eagle-eyed search, but to no avail.

'Murder, isn't it?' a smoky male voice sympathised when she sighed. 'You're not in the place five minutes before you're expected to decide whether you want to spend the next fifty-two weekends clinging to a rock-face, or spotting car numbers, or campaigning to save an endangered species.'

As Gabrielle looked up into a pair of laughing blue eyes fringed with thick black lashes, her heart took a leap. Around them swarmed a multitude of perfectly agreeable young men, but his good looks, his *sheen*, placed this one in a species all of his own. Suddenly being a student did not promise mere fun, it offered magic.

'The tap-dance ensemble is mighty tempting,' she grinned.

He made a frank appraisal of her slender body and long legs. 'In top hat and tails, you'll knock 'em dead.'

She laughed. 'But I have two left feet.'

'Nobody's perfect.'

She wasn't, Gabrielle thought. With her snub nose, generous mouth and the little-girl dimples she heartily wished she could iron out, she would answer to 'cute' or, at a pinch, 'pretty', but she did not consider herself to be one of life's beautiful people—like him. So why was he smiling as though he could not stop? Why did he look as if she had been dropped from heaven?

'In the spare moments when you're not performing the soft-shoe shuffle, what subject will you be studying?' he enquired.

Gabrielle gasped as a surge in the crowd slammed her up against him. 'Japanese, with a computer option,' she said, speaking into the depths of a cream cable-knit sweater.

He put his hands on her arms to steady her.

'But?'

'I'm not sure if it's the right choice,' she confessed, surprised to find him recognising doubts she had only belatedly owned up to herself.

'Want to talk about it?'

Gabrielle was not in the habit of confiding in strangers, but somehow he did not seem like a stranger. Somehow, he seemed like a friend.

'Yes, please,' she said.

Introductions were made on their way over to the refectory, and as they drank coffee Gabrielle told Saul O'Connor how she felt she had been brainwashed into taking Japanese, and brainwashed into attending university, if the truth were told.

'I'm an only child and my father is very ambitious for me,' she explained. 'He didn't have any further education—the money wasn't there—but for his daughter it was planned from birth. All my life seems to have been planned,' she said, with a grimace.

'University is your father's idea?' Saul asked.

'Yes. Don't get me wrong, he didn't force me or even persuade, he was just tremendously *enthusiastic*. I should have resisted, but Dad was so proud when I gained a place and——' Gabrielle sighed '—when someone's invested all their hopes and dreams in you, saying no isn't easy.'

'He suggested you study Japanese, too?'

She nodded. 'I've always done well at languages, and he considers it'll be my passport to a wonderful future. And the computer option is icing on the cake.'

'You're fortunate to have a father who's interested.' Saul gave a twisted smile. 'My old man couldn't care less. It was my uncle who insisted I stop misspending my youth and buckle down to something worth while.'

'How was your youth misspent?' Gabrielle asked, gripped with an urge to know everything there was to know about him.

'I left school at sixteen with one O level and a cloud over my head after a *liaison dangereuse* with the housemaster's daughter. Expelled,' he said, with a careless smile. 'And for the next three or four years I drifted.'

'Doing what?'

'Getting and losing dead-end jobs, attending too many rowdy parties, drinking too much.'

'Oh,' she said, feeling horribly cheated.

As he had said, nobody was perfect, but these flaws were a grave disappointment. She had expected better of him.

'Don't worry,' Saul grinned, 'you're looking at a reformed character. The bad behaviour was attention-seeking. My mother died when I was thirteen and my father promptly packed me off to boarding-school,' he explained. 'He made it plain that he was eager to get rid of me, and when he remarried six months later, I understood why. My father had never had much time for children, my mother was the cement which held our family together, but——'

'You have brothers and sisters?' Gabrielle interrupted.

'One of each, but they're ten years older than me so they'd already left home. However, after his marriage my father withdrew even further,' he continued, 'thanks to his new wife. She already had two grown-up children, and the prospect of taking on a teenage stepson did not thrill her one bit.' He moved his shoulders. 'When I went home for holidays my presence was resented and they made me feel like an outcast. Dad would supply cash by the wallet-load, but tender, loving care—no deal. At the time I would've denied it strenuously, but all the messing around and being a bad boy was my attempt to get him to notice me. It failed. Now we're virtual strangers.'

'Your uncle noticed you,' Gabrielle prompted, when he frowned and fell silent.

'Yes. Jeffrey arrived at my lodgings one day, and proceeded to put me straight in no uncertain terms! The outcome was that I enrolled at a private college, slogged through the necessary exams, and eventually took a degree in economics.'

'Your choice?'

'My choice. And now I'm doing a Ph.D., which is also of my choosing.' Saul rested an elbow on the table. 'Here I am, twenty-eight years old and still a student,' he said, with a wry smile.

'I thought you looked a fair bit older than the rest of the crowd.'

'A fair bit?' he protested. 'You make it sound as though I'm on the point of disintegration!'

'From the age of twenty-five our brain cells die off at the rate of one hundred thousand a day,' Gabrielle intoned solemnly.

'If senility is nigh, I'd better speed things up. What d'you say we have lunch, go for a walk this afternoon, spend the evening together? And drive over to the coast tomorrow?'

She had said yes, and from then on everything did proceed at top speed. A month later they were involved in a relationship which felt so easy and so right, Gabrielle knew it had been preordained. She also knew she would be staying at university—try and get her to leave!—though she didn't know whether she should stick with her Japanese.

'I still think I ought to make enquiries about what's involved if I do decide to change courses,' she said, one evening.

'And I still think you ought to wait,' Saul replied. 'You've only attended a handful of lectures, so who knows, by the end of the year——'

'The year?' she exclaimed in horror.

Again it was Saturday and, as the other girls had gone home for the weekend, they had the house to themselves. Saul was stretched out on the sofa, while she pondered her future from a beanbag on the floor.

'OK, by the end of the term you could feel differently.' He looked at her sideways. 'The young are known to change their minds.'

Gabrielle knelt forward to poke him in the ribs.

'So saith Methuselah. Oh!' she yelped, as he rolled down from the sofa, grabbed hold of her and began kissing her.

They had kissed before—frequently—but, for some reason, tonight his kisses seemed more intense. Tonight the sensations of touch and taste were heightened. Tonight Gabrielle felt as though an electrical force had invaded her body—a force which made her skin hot and tight, a force which made every nerve-end stand to attention.

When at last Saul raised his head, she saw from the heaviness of his eyes, the deep breaths he needed to take, that he was similarly disturbed. He propped himself up on his elbow and slowly traced the curve of her lips, administering love with one finger.

'Gabby,' he muttered, 'you are the most delectable, bewitching, beddable——'

Her heart jumped. 'Beddable?'

'It can't have escaped your notice that I've spent much of the last four weeks in a state of extreme arousal?'

She entwined her arms around his neck and pulled him down until he was lying almost on top of her.

'Sounds dangerous,' she murmured.

'And so's that,' Saul said, when she began

unbuttoning his shirt.

She grinned. 'You don't like it?'

'I like it, and I like you. No,' he corrected, 'I love you.'

Gabrielle gazed at him in wonderment. He loved her? This gorgeous man—the one who made her girlfriends green with envy—actually loved her? Never-never land *did* exist.

'You do?' she breathed, unable to believe her luck.

He placed a hand to his heart. 'Madly, passionately,' he declared, in senatorial tones.

'I love you, too.'

Saul gave a wide smile, and as he began kissing her again Gabrielle's belief that lovemaking belonged to those who had made a long-term and serious commitment suddenly became irrelevant. She wanted to give herself to him. She wanted to give herself to him *now*.

'Undress me,' she murmured.

He frowned. 'Gabby, I don't think——'

She leant forward, and with the tip of her tongue she outlined his lips as he had outlined hers with his finger.

'Please,' she implored.

Saul gave a muttered protest and concurred, and it was a long time before either of them achieved any further rational thought.

Gabrielle stirred drowsily. She had never imagined that making love, especially for the first time, would be so marvellous. When he had entered her it had hurt for a moment, but only a moment, for then a tornado of passion had snatched her up, whirling her around and around, sending her spinning, spinning, spinning . . .

'Why didn't you tell me you were a virgin?' Saul asked, beside her.

'I thought you would've guessed,' she said, floating on a soft white cloud.

'How?'

'I don't know.'

'So you're not on the pill or anything?' he demanded.

'Don't be cross.'

Saul stared at the ceiling. 'I'm not.'

'We love each other,' she said, certain this made everything all right.

'Yes.'

Although he had sighed, Gabrielle experienced a burst of exhilaration. Boldly she trickled her fingertips across his thigh.

'Then show me,' she said.

Droll blue eyes swung her way. 'Again?'

'I have a feeling you might be able to manage it.'

'So do I. I also have a feeling you ought to move in with me.'

'Move in?' she said, in surprise.

'Quit the house and share my flat.' He grinned. 'Two in a bed beats the hell out of sleeping alone.'

Gabrielle stepped off the cloud and placed a foot on reality. For her, living with someone would be a

major and unorthodox event—as unusual as
joining a commune of headhunters in Papua New
Guinea—but Saul appeared to take the
development for granted.

'Has—has any other girl ever shared your flat?'
she asked falteringly, feeling gauche and painfully
young.

'There's been a long procession of blondes,
brunettes, redheads—in strict rotation. I allow 'em
four months each.'

She laughed. 'And the previous girl had dark
hair? Now I know why you made a beeline for
me.'

'I like a little order in my life.' He drew her hand
lower down his thigh. 'And a little ecstasy,' he
murmured.

It did not take Gabrielle long to discover that in
Saul's world order and ecstasy often came turn and
turn about. After that rapturous night, the first
thing he did was arrange an appointment for her at
the birth control clinic.

'What do I say?' she had appealed.

He had winked. 'Tell 'em you're planning an
excessively active sex life. They'll get the
gist.'

Nights of ecstasy assured, she moved in. Saul's
flat consisted of three airy, well-furnished but
slightly neglected rooms, which had great
potential. A plant here, a poster or two there, and a
vigorous spring-cleaning would make all the
difference, Gabrielle suggested on her arrival, and

he immediately agreed. It was arranged that they would tackle the transformation together at the weekend, but the cancellation of a lecture landed her with some free time. Like a fiend, Gabrielle scrubbed and washed and polished. She bought posters, lugged back a Swiss cheese-plant, and finished the day by preparing a somewhat adventurous curry. Saul's subsequent delight in her, and hers in the changes she had wrought, were all the encouragement she needed to embark on a regime where she cleaned the flat, bought the groceries, became chief cook and bottle-washer. Gabrielle loved living with Saul. She loved looking after him. She had never been so happy in her life.

'I used to grumble like mad if my mother asked me to do the dusting, but here it's sheer pleasure,' she grinned, when he protested that there was no need for her to play housewife. 'Oh, if she could see me now.'

'But she won't, until you advise her of your change of address,' Saul pointed out.

Gabrielle frowned. Wary of her parents' reaction to the news that their precious daughter was cohabiting—and with a man she had known only a month—she had decided to maintain a 'presence' at the terraced house, in the form of a few books and clothes left in her room. With her parents unlikely to arrive unannounced, the deception was unnecessary, but it provided a breathing space. Before she dropped the bombshell in their laps, she needed to work out exactly what she would say, and how she would say it.

'I'll reveal all soon,' she promised.

'The longer you leave it, the harder it'll be,' he warned. 'Sugar, your folks might not approve, but plenty of couples live together these days.' He grinned. 'It's no big deal.'

In fact, there was little Saul rated as a big deal. Although he worked hard and long at his studies, he was one of the most relaxed people she had ever met. The master of any situation, he was also very, very funny. His wit would emerge at the most unexpected moments and send Gabrielle off into fits of laughter. But the time came when there was nothing to laugh about.

Gabrielle did not cry when the doctor confirmed that she was pregnant, she suffered an awful paralysis of the mind. What did she do? What happened next? she wondered. Numbly, she stumbled through possibilities. She could have an abortion. The baby could be born and adopted. She and Saul could get married, and raise the child as the first of their family. Why not? She might be on the young side, but he was twenty-eight. And if they were married, she could ditch her Japanese. She did not like it, anyway.

That evening she was sitting beside him, pretending to watch television while she wondered how to broach the subject, when a situation comedy about a woman expecting triplets offered up an opportunity.

'What would you say if I told you *I* was

pregnant?' Gabrielle enquired, as canned hilarity richocheted around the room.

'Goodbye.'

'Goodbye?' she echoed, gazing at his profile in dismay. The question had been a conscious toe-in-the-water exercise, but, like a piranha, he had disposed of the toe in a single bite. With one word she had been dismembered, disabled, discarded.

'Just kidding.' Saul turned from the screen. 'You're not . . . are you?'

'Yes.'

'You're having a baby?' He stared at her for what seemed like hours. 'Are you sure?' he said at last.

'I'm sure. I'm sure,' Gabrielle babbled. 'I bought one of those testing kits and it was positive, so this afternoon I went to see the doctor. It must have happened that first night.'

He ran a bemused hand through his hair. 'Why on earth didn't you say something?'

Gabrielle gave an aimless shrug. 'At first I thought maybe the upheaval of starting at university had disrupted things. I didn't feel any different, not the slightest bit, so I waited and hoped and——'

'How many weeks pregnant are you?' he interrupted.

'The doctor reckons about thirteen.'

Saul frowned. 'What do you intend to do?'

'Me?'

'Gabby, it's your body.'

Although his tone was quiet, the message came over loud and clear. Her body, but *their* baby—yet he had not said that. The onus, it seemed, was on her.

'I—I don't know,' she said, in a thin voice.

Saul placed his arm around her shoulders.

'Sugar, nothing is as bad or as awful as it seems at the time. And there are a few weeks yet before things become vital.'

Gabrielle looked down at her hands. What he meant was that there were a few weeks before she reached the deadline for an abortion.

'True,' she said abstractedly.

'Would you like a cup of coffee?' he asked.

'Please.'

Coffee, and a few comforting words, were, she realised, all she was going to be offered. Saul had not rushed to present himself as a willing, or even not-so-willing, father. He had not gone down on one knee and proposed. Resentment flared. The situation might not be vital, but it was damned important!

'You remember you told me about the housemaster's daughter?' she said, when he returned with steaming mugs. 'Did you make her pregnant?'

'For heaven's sake, no!'

Gabrielle regarded him through narrowed eyes. 'What about your other girlfriends?'

'Negative. I have never fathered a child before.'

'How do I know that?' she demanded.

Yesterday she had admired Saul's laid-back

style, now it had become an affront. She would shatter that cosmic calm. She would rile and infuriate. She would make the bastard throw things!

'Because I'm telling you,' he said firmly.

Dumping her coffee on a side-table, Gabrielle swept to her feet. Hands on hips, she glared down.

'You might not be telling me the truth!'

'Is that hole in your jeans there by accident or design?' he asked serenely. 'Whichever, when you thrust out your pelvis it provides a flash of naked skin which is unbearably sexy.'

'Hole? What hole?' she demanded, frowning down.

He leant forward and prodded with a finger. 'That one.'

'Oh.' She brushed him away. 'In the past you've said a number of things which I took to be in fun,' she continued haughtily, 'like the rota of blondes, brunettes and redheads. Now I'm beginning to wonder if what you said could've been for real!'

'Your pelvis is for real.' Saul rolled admiring eyes. 'So-o-o real.' He stood up and put his arms around her waist. 'Gabby, let's make love, not war,' he appealed.

She held herself rigid. 'You think you can charm me, but——'

'But what?' he murmured, nibbling seductively at her neck.

Gabrielle's anger evaporated. She did not want

to be coaxed or bamboozled, yet the drugging nearness of him allowed her no choice.

'But you can,' she sighed.

Over the next few days, her state of mind see-sawed erratically. Maybe hormonal changes were responsible, yet although there were times when she believed Saul genuinely cared, the feeling grew that his caring could be a sham. On the look-out for someone to share his bed he, an adult male of some experience, must have recognised her as innocent, easily swayed and, within minutes of meeting him, besotted. As for cleaning and cooking, she had come made to measure! True, he had never asked her to be his slave, he was far too clever for that. Instead Saul had massaged her emotions in such a way that she had fallen over herself trying to please him. That calm was a shrewd disguise. Behind it lurked a thundering schemer, an opportunist, a louse!

Twice Gabrielle had come from her corner with fists raised, determined to thrash out the matter, and twice he had refused to enter the ring.

'If you fancy a fight over the weekend, I'm afraid you're out of luck,' Saul said, as he replaced the phone an evening or two later. 'That was my uncle inviting me to stay.' He pulled a face. 'Jeffrey's arranged a dinner where I'm to meet some big men from big companies.'

So, by the time he completed his thesis next summer, the old boys' network would have guaranteed him a job? Gabrielle was not surprised. The sheen she had noticed the first time they had met had long since been recognised as the sheen of privilege. Saul's father was a wealthy landowner, and his uncle—so it had transpired—was none other than the famous business magnate and multi-millionaire, Sir Jeffrey O'Connor. There were no titled gents in her family, she thought wryly, and not much surplus cash, either.

'How long will you be away?' she asked.

'Three nights.' He came and put his arms around her. 'Will you be all right on your own? You could always sleep at the house with the girls.'

'I'll be fine here,' she assured him.

It was Saturday afternoon when Gabrielle became aware of odd little cramps at the top of her thighs. They continued off and on into the evening, though she did not know why. All she could think of was that it had poured the previous day, and in her haste to get out of the rain she had run several marathons from one lecture-room to the next. The cramps did not feel like strained muscles, but perhaps that was what she had done. Then she found a dot of blood on her panties. She stared at it in alarm. What did it mean? Was it important? Should she call the doctor?

When Saul rang ten minutes later, she was delirious with gratitude. At garbled length, she told him about the rain, the cramps, how she needed his advice.

'A dot?' he queried, and in the background she heard the buzz of conversation and laughter. Clearly, the dinner was an unqualified success.

'A tiny spot.'

'It doesn't sound like anything to worry about,' Saul said.

'You're right,' Gabrielle agreed, embarrassed by her infantile panic.

There he was, dressed in a dinner-jacket, discussing sophisticated matters in sophisticated company. And here she was, in her old towelling dressing-gown, yattering away like a moron.

'Have a glass of something and a warm bath, and tuck yourself up in bed,' he suggested. 'A good night's sleep should do the trick.'

When he had rung off, she looked in the drinks cupboard. They had finished the wine, all that remained was a half-bottle of gin. Gabrielle drank one gin and tonic, and decided to have another. When she was in the middle of her bath, the water began to stain with red. She summoned the doctor. The doctor summoned an ambulance. Less than an hour after she arrived in hospital, she had miscarried.

The doctor and the nurses seemed to believe that, in view of her youth and unmarried state, she had reason to be grateful.

'No damage done. You'll be able to produce strapping sons and daughters in the future,' she was told bracingly.

Gabrielle gave a brave smile but, left alone, she sobbed despairingly into her pillow. At the beginning of the day a baby had been growing inside her. Its little heart had been beating. Its tiny fingers and toes had been forming. Now that baby was dead. How could she ever have been so cruel, so unfeeling, as to consider an abortion?

The next day she went back to the flat. Saul rang and when she told him what had happened, he caught the next train home.

'Sugar, it's probably for the best,' he soothed, as tears washed down her cheeks.

'That's—that's what they said at the hospital.'

'It's all over now,' he murmured consolingly.

She took a shuddering breath. 'I suppose so.'

Weeks passed, yet although the doctor pronounced her fit Gabrielle felt exhausted. Every ounce of energy was needed to drag herself to lectures and drag herself back again. Why she bothered was unclear. She did not care about the lectures, or anything else. All she cared about was the baby. Losing it had become a burden of personal anguish she carried with her day and night.

She tried to talk about it to Saul, but he always switched to another subject—like describing his dinner with the bigwigs and, later, telling her about a job he had obtained with the White Group. To hear him talk, the two events were unrelated, but Gabrielle was not deceived. She knew he had capitalised on his family connections.

Neither was she deceived by his refusal to speak about the baby. Although, admittedly, at first she had thought he might be avoiding the topic in order to hasten her recovery—least said, soonest mended—it soon dawned that his lack of interest was just that. He could joke, shine bright, be so ruthlessly *trivial*, because the baby meant nothing to him. He had not cared about it at the start. He did not care now. He was *glad* it had died.

Gabrielle realised she must leave him—why she had stayed this long with such a glib, self-centred, unfeeling monster she did not know—yet when it came to moving back into the house the thought of the effort involved proved too much. As housework and lovemaking were also too much for her, why Saul did not send *her* packing seemed equally strange. She had ceased to be of use to him, plus she had overrun the allotted four-month stay! Perhaps he felt it would be bad for his image to turf out a girl so obviously frail? Perhaps all he was waiting for was the first sign of a spring in her step, and then her luggage would be flung on to the street as he waved a hasty goodbye. He would have no difficulty finding another bedmate, another stooge. Perhaps he already had a blonde lined up?

Trudging home one afternoon, Gabrielle found herself considering, yet again, the events which had led up to the miscarriage when—abruptly, agonisingly—she realised *why* it had happened. She stopped dead. Saul had given instructions and she, being weak and silly and inclined to believe he knew best, had followed them to the letter!

'You killed my baby,' Gabrielle flung at him, the moment she walked in the door. She stomped across to his desk, where he was writing.

'You never wanted it, so you decided to kill it!'

Saul twisted the cap back on to his pen and placed the papers inside a folder. 'I need to see my tutor,' he said heavily. 'We'll discuss this later.'

'Discuss?' she sneered. 'We've never discussed *anything* remotely connected with my pregnancy. Surely you don't intend to——?'

'I don't intend to let you get away with that accusation!' he shot back, then drew in a steadying breath. 'We'll discuss this later,' he repeated, 'when you've calmed down.'

After he had gone, Gabrielle wandered around the rooms. Saul had sounded sincere about talking things over—at long last—but . . . but . . . but. She resented the idea that everything hinged on *her* regaining her composure. She resented being left to hang around until he returned. She resented his manipulation. Once she might have been cravenly adoring, now——

Impetuously, she phoned for a taxi, filled it with her belongings, then went round to the terraced house and collected what remained from there. By the nightfall she was back home with her parents, and by the end of the week she had moved down to London. Her days as a student had ended. Her romance was over.

Yet, although she had removed herself from his presence, she could not remove Saul from her mind. Gabrielle knew it was foolish but, for months, whenever the phone rang, whenever she

received letters, she wondered if *today* he
might get in touch. He did not. As the baby had
failed to stir his attention, so, it was heart-
wrenchingly obvious, had she!

CHAPTER FOUR

GABRIELLE gave a groan of frustration. Never mind the complexities of building up a business. Forget about simultaneously controlling a dozen shops. They were child's play compared to the installation of an Austrian blind! Church bells had been summoning worshippers to morning service when she had first removed the lemon-flowered gauze from its cellophane and read the 'simple' instructions, but by now everyone must have eaten their Sunday lunch. Everyone except her. She raised herself on tiptoe, poked the screwdriver behind the curtain track and, in a herculean effort, attempted to loosen it again. For the umpteenth time, the screw refused to budge. She knew why: her angle of attack was wrong. The top of the window ran close to the ceiling and, with the added complication of being sited over the sink, the track was not easily accessible. To achieve the required grip, she needed to be three inches taller. Muttering choice words, she clambered down from the draining-board and on to a chair, off the chair and on to the floor. Gabrielle wiped her hands on the seat of her jeans. A banana and a carton of toffee yoghurt were unlikely to add extra height, but they could provide extra 'get up and go'. And if she got up far enough . . .

As she ate, she began to brood. Three days had been devoted to examining and re-examining Saul's comments on 'minor parts being sacrificed to save the major,' and what had she decided? Nothing. Every aspect of what he might do with Anniversaries had been considered, yet each was pure conjecture. Until the marauding tiger actually sprang, she could not shackle him. But shackle him she would, or expire in the attempt! Whether he intended to dispose of her company *en bloc* or in bits, or if it was not to be sold but restricted to its present size—a lesser but none the less repugnant threat—Gabrielle was determined to be prepared. All eventualities would be investigated and appropriate tactics planned. For example, the minutiae of the complex contract which tied her to Betancourts must be scanned. Were there loopholes to be found in the fine print, maybe in the form of some kind of buy-back clause? The likelihood seemed remote, and she did not possess sufficient capital to repurchase her shares in any case, but—well, there must be financiers who could be inveigled into coming to the rescue. She gave a wan smile. At the time of drawing up the contract she had, she recalled, blithely told Kevin that as *he* was the one with the eye for such details *he* should get on with it. Always impatient with the nuts and bolts of paperwork, Gabrielle conceded that such a lack of interest had been a mistake. Now she must educate herself. If Saul did see her shops as a bunch of assets which were worth more broken up, she would need something far stronger than her partner's affable support to bind him. Kevin might be loyal, but when it came to pinioning down a dangerous animal she had to doubt his stamina.

The banana skin was discarded and the foil lid pealed from her yoghurt. Saul could not instigate a raid on her business overnight, nor without first approaching her, so this week at home would be spent allowing ideas to percolate, be tasted, and the choicest to be refined. Until next Monday she would—thoughts apart—remain strictly inoperative. She did not intend to rush in and pre-empt the issue; that way lay disaster.

Gabrielle pushed a straggle of hair from her eyes. Although inoperative in the business world, at home she intended to be relentlessly on the go. Already she had started. From the crack of dawn she had been scrubbing out cupboards, wiping down paintwork, cleaning windows. She licked the yoghurt from her spoon and gazed contentedly around. Progress had been made. Maybe she was as filthy as sin and had broken every fingernail, but the kitchen sparkled. Once the blind had been fixed, the room would be a sheer delight. Once the blind had been fixed, she would welcome in tour parties. But how did she fix it?

One solution would be to construct a platform of books—and risk a tumble. Another, to plead help from the gentleman who lived next door. Yes? No? With a Daimler in the garage and a plummy voice,

he was awe-inspiringly grand. Could he be one of
the one hundred and eighty-four peers reputed to
live in the Royal Borough? she wondered. She did
not know, she had only spoken to him twice. But
they were neighbours, Gabrielle thought, and
whenever he saw her he smiled. For someone of the
right height, hanging the blind would not take
long. The favour did not seem too much to
ask—did it? The doorbell rang, shrilling into the
silence and making her jump. Who was this?
Everyone at the office had been told she was
unconditionally incommunicado, so could her
prayers have been answered and her neighbour was
coming to call?

On winged feet, Gabrielle sped to the door. With
a hopeful smile, she opened it.

'Oh,' she said.

Her visitor's eyes travelled from her loose and
tangled hair to her grimy yellow sweatshirt, to
the purple ribbed tights, to her large red fuzzy
slippers.

'Be still my heart!' Saul declared, clutching
wildly at his chest.

Her instinct was to laugh, or stick out her
tongue—until she recalled the damage he had once
done, and could do.

'Amanda also told you where I live?' she said
frostily. Now reminded of what a mess she must
look, Gabrielle was relieved no member of the
aristocracy had decided to pop round.

'She did, and as I happened to be in your
neighbourhood I thought I'd stop by for a few

minutes.' Saul hesitated. 'But I see you're busy.'

'Very.'

'Another time, then.'

As he turned to go, she stared at him in his navy sweater and jeans, and it registered that her visitor stood tall, tall, *tall*.

'Wait. Are you any good at screwing?' Gabrielle enquired impulsively.

He threw back his head and laughed. 'If you don't remember, then modesty restrains me——'

'What I meant was, could you help me take down a curtain rail and convert it to carry an Austrian blind?' she explained, hot colour racing up her neck.

'I could try.'

In the kitchen he deftly removed the rail, put the brackets and cord eyes in place, then refixed the rail.

'Pass me the blind and I'll hang it on the track,' he offered. Legs apart to accommodate the sink, Saul was balanced with one foot on the drainer and the other on the corner work-surface. A scant two yards by three, the kitchen with its wall-to-wall units allowed minimum room for manoeuvre. 'You'll need to say if the gathers are even,' he told her.

As Gabrielle came closer, her pulse started to race. Her standpoint on the floor gave a close-up view of denimed legs which seemed to go on forever, of strong thighs, of his neat backside. Eight years ago, she would have reached up and patted it, and he would have laughed and said something. Probably something obscene. Something which would have ended up with them rolling around on the floor together, or on the couch, or in bed. Their relationship might have been pot-holed for the last few weeks, but prior to that it had been . . . bliss?

'That suit?' Saul enquired, gravely arranging the ruches.

'Er——' the blind received a swift inspection '—it's fine. Thank you very much.'

'Strange as it may seem, I've enjoyed fixing that,' he grinned, as he jumped down. 'In the States I rented serviced apartments, so it's years since I've done anything remotely domestic. It felt good.' He rested a hip against the cooker. 'Remember those bookshelves I built when we lived together?'

Gabrielle told herself to take it calmly, take it coolly, to be matter of fact—like him.

'I remember how you bored everyone senseless talking about them!'

'They were state of the art,' he protested, in mock outrage. 'How about me building you some shelves today, or maybe plumbing in a jacuzzi or retiling the roof?'

This time she did laugh. She could not help herself. 'No, thanks.'

'There's nothing else I can do?'

Gabrielle dithered. Inviting him into her home in the first place did not rate as entirely prudent—play hostess to a tiger, and you could get scratched. So wasn't becoming further beholden

just another foolhardy step? Maybe, and yet——
She had a long list of jobs which required brute
strength, but with her parents abroad on holiday it
would be at least another three weeks before her
father could possibly come and help.

'The removal men left a chest of drawers in the
garage and I'd like it in the spare room,' she said.
'Do you think——?'

'Let's go.'

Together they carried the drawers up the stairs.
Next Saul shifted a wardrobe from one side of her
bedroom to the other, and as he was so ready,
willing and able she asked if he could please
move a filing-cabinet into the study, and
re-site the sideboard and sofa in the living-
room.

'That's much better!' Gabrielle declared
happily, when everything had been rearranged.

He stood in the doorway, one hand gripping
either side of the frame. 'Looks great,' he agreed,
panting from his exertions.

'It'll look even greater when I can afford new
furniture.'

Saul's eyes circled the white-painted walls, the
Cotswold stone fireplace, the latticed windows,
then he looked behind him down the hall.

'Even so, you already have a very attractive
home here.'

'Thanks,' she beamed, unreasonably pleased
by his praise. 'And thanks for all your help.'

He made a dismissive gesture. 'As soon as I have
the time, I'll need to start looking for a place

myself. I'm in a hotel at the moment, but there's a
limit to how much living out of a suitcase anyone
can stand.' Saul grimaced. 'Mind you, from the
advertisements I've seen, London properties
appear to cost the earth these days.'

'And half the moon, though if you're lucky
you might manage to pick up a bargain. I did.
Would you like a lager?' Gabrielle suggested,
when he drew his fingers across a sweat-glossed
brow.

'Please. How did you find this bargain of
yours?' he asked, going with her to the kitchen.

She handed him a can from the fridge and took
one for herself. 'Sheer luck. I'd always hankered
after a mews house, and I happened to spot details
of this place in the paper. It sounded ideal,
though far too expensive. However, it was near
the Kensington shop which made calling in easy,
and I thought it would be sensible to check out
what was available for the price, for future
reference.'

'In other words, you were nosey,' Saul stated,
ripping off the ring-pull and taking several greedy
swigs.

Gabrielle grinned. 'Yes. Viewing was by
appointment, but I took a chance and paid an
impromptu visit, and the young couple who owned
it, a Mr and Mrs Adler, were delighted to show me
around. First thing the next morning, a woman
from the estate agents was on the phone, asking for
my reaction. I told her I thought the house was
fantastic, but confessed that although I had funds

available they didn't equal the sum required. She suggested I take out a mortgage to make up the shortfall, but I wasn't keen on saddling myself with hefty monthly repayments.'

'Even so, it sounds as though you must have accumulated a fair amount of cash,' he observed.

'I had. Because I'd lived in the same rented flat in the same grotty area ever since I came to London, my outgoings had been low. Also, I'm not in the habit of swanning off to Barbados or treating myself to jewellery, nor do I drive a car, so——' Gabrielle shrugged '—my savings just grew and grew.'

He gestured towards the fridge. 'Mind if I have another lager?'

'Do.'

'And what you offered the Adlers was enough?' Saul prompted, as they carried their cans through to the living-room.

She nodded. 'It was way below the asking-price, but the agent said she'd refer back even so. To my amazement the Adlers accepted; on condition the cash was in their hands within a fortnight.'

Saul sat down in an armchair, legs thrown wide apart. 'Why the urgency?'

'Heaven knows. The agent's theory was that they must have come a cropper with shares and been cleaned out, but they'd only moved in here themselves just before Christmas, so their downfall seems to have been very sudden.'

'Did they go to a less expensive area?' he asked,

as he drank his beer.

'I've no idea. They didn't leave a forwarding address, nor tell any of the neighbours their destination. I called round a couple of days before the deal was final in the hope of having a chat and a further look around, but the house was empty.'

'The Adlers had already quit?'

'Yes. Apparently as soon as they knew the money was firm, they were——' Gabrielle's hand sketched a rising jet '—up, up and away. On the actual transfer day Mr Adler arrived at the solicitors to collect the cheque in person. He cleared it within an hour.'

'Odd,' Saul said thoughtfully.

'Another oddity is the number of things they left behind them. The deal included carpets, light fittings, kitchen appliances, et cetera, but when I opened the freezer it was full of food.' She indicated a bonsai tree which grew in an earthenware pot on the sideboard. 'All the house plants around the place are theirs, and the wrought-iron table and chairs, the urns, the pair of lions on the patio, also came courtesy of the Adlers.'

Saul went to look out of the french windows which opened on to a small walled square at the rear of the house. 'Those lions are beautiful. Are they bronze?'

'I think so. I found a drawer crammed with sheets and pillow-cases, brand new and in the original wrapping,' she continued 'and something at the back of almost every cupboard, particularly on the high shelves. When I realised how many items were involved I rang the agent, but she hadn't a clue where the Adlers had gone, either. I keep expecting them to arrive on the doorstep and say, ''Please can we have our chicken Kiev and our lions?'' But it hasn't happened yet.'

'Leaving so much stuff doesn't tie in with them being strapped for cash,' he said, coming to sit beside her on the sofa.

'I know. The man who runs the fruit stall on the corner told me that the Adlers moved out in two hours flat, so it seems as though they grabbed whatever was in clear sight and didn't bother too much about the rest.'

'Strange people,' he commented.

That she should be relaxed in his company, now *that* was strange, Gabrielle thought, suddenly realising how close they were sitting, how she had been generously sharing confidences, how the past half-hour had seemed so much like the old times—the good old times.

'What brought you round here this afternoon?' she asked, vowing not to be so garrulous or unguarded again.

'I came because——' Saul hesitated. 'You told me you didn't go on Caribbean holidays,' he said slowly. 'How about kicking up autumn leaves, or running barefoot along a seashore, or staying in bed late at the weekends?'

Gabrielle frowned, unsure where he was leading. 'I haven't done any of those lately, but——'

'You did once,' he interrupted. There was a tear in the knee of her tights, and he reached out to rub the tip of his finger back and forth across the patch of exposed skin. 'Don't you think you could be in danger of losing sight of life's more spontaneous pleasures?'

She sat very still. Could this be why he had dropped by—to ask questions which, no doubt by a circuitous route, would go from persuading her that the life she led was far too hectic, to the insistence that, for her own sake, she must ease off, to a declaration that the demise of Anniversaries would be a blessing in disguise? Was he here today to start a softening-up and prising-away process? And, if so, should she pretend to go along with what he said, or did she vehemently object?

'Maybe,' she replied cautiously.

Saul grinned. 'Y'know, I like this Orphan Annie look of yours.'

She stared down at the golden finger which stroked her knee. As circuitous routes went, this one threatened to be more serpentine than most—already he had lost her.

'And for your next joke?' Gabrielle said drily.

'It's the lily-white truth! Seeing you so outwardly scruffy reminds me of how clean and smooth and silky you always were——' he pushed his finger beneath the purple ribbing '—under your clothes.'

As he ventured on to previously unexplored skin, her heart started to pound. He was touching a most prosaic area, and yet she felt as if he were caressing hidden, erotic places. Her erstwhile lover always had had a knack of disarming her, of seducing her, and, maddeningly, she realised she was still susceptible.

'As you said, the past is gone,' she declared stiffly. 'So——'

'I was wrong. The past is always with us, Peters,' Saul murmured. 'And the thought of you beneath your clothes reminds me of how——' All of a sudden, his head shot up and his eyes narrowed. He leapt to his feet. 'What the hell's going on?' he demanded.

In the doorway stood two men in black tracksuits, with knitted balaclavas over their heads. Gabrielle goggled at them in astonishment. How long had they been there? What were they doing? Where had they come from?

The shorter of the pair, a beefy individual, made a curt gesture towards Saul.

'Hold it right there,' he growled, in a thick Scottish accent.

Gabrielle gasped. The man was carrying a gun! This isn't real, her mind decided. It couldn't be. She was watching a film. Or, instead of sending a gorilla-gram, some jester at the office had decided to surprise her with two men dressed up as burglars. Yes, that must be it. And, to make the joke even better, one man came squat and barrel-shaped, while the other loomed tall and skinny.

She was tempted to laugh, but as the intruder stepped forward any amusement died in her throat. Only his eyes were visible, yet the menace she saw in them told her this was no joke. This was in deadly earnest.

'Do as I say,' he rasped, 'and nobody'll get hurt.'

'That's very comforting,' Saul replied, showing remarkable cool. 'But what is it you want?'

Unsteadily, Gabrielle pushed herself upright. 'Unless you're interested in a four-year-old television and—and a pair of bronze lions,' she gulped, 'there's nothing of value here.'

The bruiser snorted. 'Is that so?'

'Yes, it is!' she said, annoyed by his brusque tone. Even if he had taken the liberty of illegally entering her home, he could at least be civil. 'How did you get in?' Gabrielle demanded.

The tall man, who appeared to be younger—maybe in his early twenties—giggled nervously.

'Through the skylight on the landing. I'm afraid we've mucked up your ceiling.'

She visualised the once pristine ivory paper now smeared with black. 'Of all the lousy, low-down tricks!' she protested. 'How dare you break into my house and——?'

'Would you care to tell us exactly what it is you've come for?' Saul asked again.

The Scot took over as spokesman. 'It's not what we've come for, big boy, it's what Mr Vincent requires.'

'Mr Vincent? Who's he?'

'Funny!' The gun twitched. 'On your way.'

Saul folded his arms. 'On my way to where?' he demanded, remaining resolutely immobile.

'You don't imagine we'd tell you that?'

'You—you mean you're not here to steal anything?' Gabrielle asked, trying desperately to work out what was happening.

'Just you.'

'Me?'

'You and 'im,' the younger man defined.

Saul frowned. 'Far be it from me to spoil your day, but I strongly suspect you guys have come to the wrong address.'

'We've got a real comedian here,' the Scot said sourly.

'This is number seven,' Gabrielle explained, at speed. 'Number seven, Garden of——'

'We know, Rita, we know.'

'Rita?' She gave a tremulous hoot. 'You *are* at the wrong address. I'm not——'

'Cut the chat.' He swung an impatient arm at Saul. 'You—*walk*.'

For a second time, Saul refused to move. 'There's been a mistake,' he insisted.

The muzzle of the gun was jabbed into his side.

'The only mistake'll be if you don't get through that door now,' the Scot threatened.

For a moment Saul seemed ready to argue again, then, with a sigh and a downward glance at the revolver, he walked into the hall.

'Who is it you're looking for?' Gabrielle implored.

The bruiser jerked his head. 'And you.'

'Is it the Adlers?' she asked, scuttling out.

'Adlers or Arnotts, you've still done the dirty on Mr Vincent,' jeered the Scot.

'I beg your pardon?'

'The boss knows all about you changing your name,' the younger man said, behind her.

'You mean Mr and Mrs Adler were—were really called Arnott?' she faltered.

'What a clever girl!' the Scot harumphed nastily.

'But the Adlers, Arnotts, whatever they're called, have gone!' Gabrielle insisted, directing her words back over her shoulder because the younger man seemed more open to reason. 'They sold this place to me a month ago.'

'Mr Vincent warned us you was a pair of tricky devils,' muttered the Scot.

'But they did!'

'She's telling the truth,' Saul said sharply.

The gun jolted into him again. 'Belt up!'

Saul ignored the intimidation. 'Have you been told what the people you're seeking are supposed to look like?' he questioned. 'Do they look like us?'

'Identical!' the Scot claimed, so hastily and so belligerently that Gabrielle was sure he had been given no description.

'Let me get my cheque-book, that'll prove my identity,' she said, all in a breath. 'It's in my bag in the study. You can look at my letters, as well. And the gas bill, and——'

The intruder stopped and turned, raising a fist the size of a ham. 'If you don't shut your mouth, I'll bloody well shut it for you!'

She flinched. Saul tensed.

'You try that,' he warned, his blue eyes glittering, 'and I'll——'

The gun was positioned over his heart.

'You'll what?'

'We overheard your husband calling you Rita,' the younger man interjected, sounding almost apologetic.

'No, no,' Gabrielle jabbered, in desperation. 'You didn't get it right. He said *Peters*. Peters is my surname and he said it as—as a joke. And he's not my husband, he's——'

'Pull the other one,' snapped the Scot, but his accomplice frowned.

'If you're not Rita Arnott, then who are you?' He gestured with a thumb. 'And who's he?'

Relief made her weak. At last her message had penetrated. At last these bully boys would understand their blunder. At last this nightmare would end.

'I'm——'

'Full marks for trying, sugar,' Saul cut in suddenly, 'but I reckon it's time we came clean.'

Her head whipped round and she gazed at him. There was a message written in his eyes, but as far as Gabrielle was concerned it might as well have been in Sanskrit.

'Come clean?' she echoed blankly.

'Whatever you say, these gentlemen aren't going to believe you . . .' he paused, then added '. . . Rita.'

CHAPTER FIVE

BEING driven along inside an ancient van which had a bare floor, no seats and neither springs nor shock absorbers was not Gabrielle's idea of fun. She felt like a peanut being shaken around in a tin can.

'Ouch!' she complained, when an extra hard bounce lifted her up and bumped her down on her backside.

'Are you all right?' Saul enquired, beside her.

She glared at him through the half-light. 'Never better,' she said, rubbing hard. 'There's nothing I enjoy more than to be kidnapped, and bruised black and blue. What a pity we're not bound and gagged; now that really would be exhilarating!'

'Whatever turns you on,' he murmured.

'Want to know one thing which doesn't? You! Isn't it about time you revealed your strategy?' Gabrielle demanded. 'I never took a degree and learned how to think logically, remember? So I'd be grateful if you would explain the reasoning which lay behind assuring those two goons that we are, indeed, the couple they were looking for.'

Saul shot a glance at the metal partition which separated the interior of the van from the cab. Near the top, in the middle, was a small window, but so far neither man had looked through. After slamming and locking the doors they appeared to have pushed their cargo to the back of their minds—for the time being.

'I don't know anything about the Adlers—Arnotts, I guess we'd better stick with Arnott from now on,' he said, speaking over a cacophony of rattles and thuds, 'but I do know a significant amount about you and me. I know that the media's splashed your name around as being the ultra-successful and, by inference, ultra-rich young woman who's created Anniversaries. I'm also aware that some people would be quick to fasten on to my connection with my uncle.'

'You reckon that makes us vulnerable?'

'Vulnerable as in valuable. To the unscrupulous, it must put us high in the ransom stakes. I'd be surprised if we don't offer manifestly richer pickings than the Arnotts.'

Gabrielle considered what he had said, then frowned. 'That's pure guesswork.'

'Well . . . yes,' he agreed reluctantly.

'Your idea is that when this Mr Vincent realises the error, he'll simply send us on our way—without bothering to find out who we are?'

'I expect he'll ask our names, but when he does we give false ones. You could say you're——' Saul undertook a mental search '—Amanda, for example, and I'll be——'

'Elvis Presley?' she cut in witheringly. 'Suppose it doesn't work like that? Suppose this Mr Vincent is interested in the Adlers—oops, Arnotts, and *only* the Arnotts? And suppose when he finds out we've impersonated them, he cuts up rough, wants to know why, and forces our real names out of us?'

Pensively he kneaded his lower lip between a forefinger and his thumb. 'Mmm,' he said.

'Didn't think of that, did you? Huh, chances are if you'd let me explain our true identities our friends through there——' Gabrielle glanced at the peephole '—would, one, have believed me, and, two, heard no bells ring. Or if they had, they still wouldn't have cared.'

'And then they would have walked away?'

'Sprinted.'

Saul shook his head. 'The gangly one might have been swayed, but not his mate. He wouldn't have the imagination. He was programmed to collect a couple from your address, and collect them he would—did—regardless.'

'You don't *know* that!'

'I know it's hellish risky to announce that you're a big-shot businesswoman and I'm the nephew of a millionaire. Or do I? Maybe I don't. I'm losing this argument, aren't I?' He ran a confused hand through his hair. 'Agreeing we were the Arnotts seemed like a good idea at the time,' he said savagely. 'Fine, so maybe in the heat of the moment I made the wrong decision, said the wrong thing—but when some thug's pressing a gun in your guts, you don't take time off to think everything the whole way through!'

Gabrielle sighed. 'I suppose not,' she agreed. She wrapped her arms around her knees and rested her head. 'Of course,' she muttered, unable to stop airing her grievances, 'we wouldn't be sitting here if you hadn't called me Peters.'

'Neither would we be here if you'd had your damned burglar alarm switched on!'

'Oh,' she said, in dawning surprise. 'No. I wondered why the Arnotts needed such a fancy system, and I suppose now I know.'

'It would seem so,' he agreed flatly.

For a few minutes they sat in silence, being jiggled and juggled around.

'I'm going to take a squint through the peephole,' Saul decided. 'Our friends must have removed their balaclavas by now, and I'd like to see what they look like. Also, with luck, I might be able to recognise where we are.'

Cautiously, he made his way forward and crouched to one side of the window. A hand on the floor to steady himself, he was rising up on his haunches when the van suddenly swerved. Knocked off balance, he crashed noisily against the metal partition, swore, and struggled to right himself. Someone glanced back, and seconds later the window was obscured with an anorak. Half-light had become gloom.

'One brilliant idea bites the dust,' Saul said ruefully, as he crawled back on all

Take 4 Medical Romances

Mills & Boon Medical Romances capture the excitement, intrigue and emotion of the busy medical world. A world often interrupted by love and romance...

We will send you 4 BRAND NEW MEDICAL ROMANCES absolutely FREE plus a cuddly teddy bear and a surprise mystery gift, as your introduction to this superb series.

At the same time we'll reserve a subscription for you to our Reader Service. Every two months you could receive the 6 latest Medical Romances delivered direct to your door POST AND PACKING FREE, plus a free Newsletter packed with competitions, author news and much, much more.

What's more there's no obligation, you can cancel or suspend your subscription at any time. So you've nothing to lose and a whole world of romance to gain!

FREE

Reader Service
FREEPOST
PO Box 236
Croydon
Surrey
CR9 9EL

SEND NO MONEY NOW

FREE BOOKS CERTIFICATE

YES please send me my 4 FREE Medical Romances, together with my
Teddy and mystery gift. Please also reserve a special Reader Service
subscription for me. If I decide to subscribe, I shall receive 6 new books every
two months for just £8.10, post and packaging free. If I decide not to
subscribe, I shall write to you within 10 days. The free books and
gifts will be mine to keep in any case.

I understand that I am under no obligation
whatsoever – I can cancel or suspend my subscription
at any time simply by writing to you.
I am over 18 years of age.

EXTRA BONUS

We all love surprises, so as well as the FREE
books and Teddy, here's an intriguing mystery gift
especially for you. No clues - send off today!

1AOD

Mrs/Miss/Ms
(Block capitals please)

Address _____

_____ Postcode _____

Signature _____

fours.

'And what do you propose now?' Gabrielle demanded. 'What's your next masterstroke?'

He sat beside her. 'We gather clues.'

'Clues like what?'

'Whenever the van stops we must listen out for any sounds which might indicate the route we're taking.' He peered at his watch. 'And by keeping a check on the time—we've been on the move almost fifteen minutes—we might be able to get a rough idea of where it is we eventually end up.'

Gabrielle slid him a worried glance. 'You reckon that kind of information's going to be crucial?'

'No way,' he said dismissively, 'but it'll make me feel as though we're doing something.'

'You'd be doing something if you attempted to break open the doors,' she mumbled.

'Gabby—Peters,' Saul adjusted, 'if you would care to take a look at——'

'OK, OK, you win. Call me Gabby,' she bit out, begrudgingly.

He grinned. 'Nothing would please me more than to be your hero of the moment, Gabby, but it'd take a battering ram to demolish the back of the van.'

She thought again. 'How about us thumping on the sides the next time we stop?'

'And give boyo an opportunity to use that gun? He's probably nowhere near as trigger-happy as he appears, but I'd prefer not to test him. How about you?'

'I guess not,' she agreed disconsolately.

Shoulders hunched, Gabrielle stared at the floor. The first surprise had gone, and the full extent of the calamity was beginning to sink in. Kidnaps were nothing new, she mused—they were a regular occurrence in Beirut, Ireland, even in London—but she had never, ever imagined she would be a victim. Recollections of hijacks, abductions, people held hostage for years, began to bang around in her head.

'Do you feel cold?' Saul asked, when she shivered.

She gave a tepid smile. 'A bit.'

'Here.' He pulled his sweater off over his head. 'Wear this.'

Gabrielle eyed his thin cotton shirt. 'But what about you?'

'Don't you remember?' he said, with a mischievous grin. 'I'm hot-blooded.'

Folding back the too-long sleeves, she marvelled that his sense of humour could remain intact, even now. 'Aren't you scared?' she asked.

'My shoes are awash with sweat, and it's all I can do not to suck my thumb.' Saul placed his arm around her shoulders. 'Don't worry. When this guy Vincent sees us, he'll arrange for us to be dropped off somewhere, then a Good Samaritan will appear, and before you know it we'll be surrounded by reporters and hauled into the television studios to relate our adventures on the six o'clock news.'

'I'd rather it was the nine o'clock edition,

because then I could change first.' Gabrielle looked down at her feet. 'Any street-cred I have would disappear forever if it became known I'd been kidnapped in my slippers.'

He raised his brows at the red fuzz. 'And what slippers!'

She giggled. 'Suppose the camera panned to my tights?' she said, suddenly feeling better.

'Nationwide hysteria,' he declared. 'The switchboard would be jammed with calls from old men frothing at the mouth.'

'You never know, I might start a new fashion. The slob look,' Gabrielle chuckled, enjoying this break in the tension, the unexpected hilarity.

'Could turn the clothing industry upside-down,' Saul agreed. His expression grew thoughtful. 'Were you expecting anyone to visit or telephone you this afternoon?' he asked.

'No.'

'So, if it should happen that we're not released today, you won't be missed until tomorrow morning when you fail to turn up at work?'

'I wouldn't be missed then. I've taken a week off and told everyone I'm not to be disturbed,' she explained.

'A week off. That's unusual, isn't it?'

'Very,' Gabrielle replied, but refused to be drawn.

'Will your parents try to make contact?' he enquired.

'No. They're away on holiday. What's the

situation with you?'

Saul massaged the back of his neck. 'I was supposed to be driving over to Bristol this evening to spend a few days at the printing works, but I warned the manager my visit could be subject to change so he's not going to bother if I don't appear.'

'What about Dana Kelham?' Gabrielle asked.

'What about her?' he replied, and she heard something defensive and prickly in his tone.

'I just thought that—that the two of you might keep in constant touch,' she said awkwardly.

'Not now.' He frowned at a change in the engine note. 'We're slowing down.'

When the van halted, Gabrielle strained to listen. She heard the thrum of other vehicles, a distant ambulance siren, a woman scolding a child—and the hoot of a river-boat.

'I think we're crossing a bridge over the Thames,' Saul said, as they set off again. 'There are traffic lights before some of them, which would explain the stop, and now we're going up a slight incline.' He squinted at his watch. 'That would tie in with our travelling-time from Kensington, too.'

'So we're heading south—yuppy-do!' she sighed, as the van speeded up. 'I wish we'd hurry up and arrive at our destination. But not yet,' Gabrielle amended, sitting straighter. 'First we must decide whose identity it is we're going to assume, just in case Mr Vincent does ask searching questions.'

* * *

By the time the van finally came to rest, their adopted personae had been honed to perfection. Both were a mix of fact and fiction—in order to avoid inadvertently landing anyone else in trouble.

'But we play everything by ear,' Saul had insisted. 'We only embark on these lies if the circumstances leave us no other option. Agreed?'

Gabrielle had nodded.

When the engine was switched off and the slam of doors indicated a joint exit from the cab, they looked at each other.

'Time of journey?' she enquired, with a shaky attempt at a smile.

'Two hours, five minutes.' He squeezed her hand. 'We'll soon be free.'

There was the crunch of gravel, the turn of a handle, and the back doors were opened wide. Gabrielle looked out eagerly, but the winter afternoon was well advanced into dusk and all she could see were grey shadows.

'Out!' barked an all-too-familiar Scottish voice. 'The lass first.'

She crawled forward and clambered down. Painfully, she straightened. 'My poor back,' she began, then shrieked with alarm as a brown paper carrier bag was dropped over her head.

The next moment, hands clasped her upper arms from behind and she was marched forwards. Disorientated, Gabrielle stumbled and would have sprawled headlong if the hands had not held her upright.

'Easy does it,' said the younger man, and he paused to allow her to regain her balance.

She had started to walk again when, from behind, she heard a ringing 'thwack', followed by a muttered protest from Saul. She stopped in her tracks.

'What's happening?' Gabrielle demanded.

'Nothing,' said her escort.

'Nothing? You don't expect me to believe that!' she remonstrated, as he moved her on.

A moment later, a second 'thwack' and a second protest gave evidence that something was definitely happening. Something violent. Something nasty. Her blood ran cold. Back at the mews, fear of noise would have held the Scot's baser instincts in check, but such constraints had gone and now he was flexing his muscles.

'Don't try to get clever with me, big boy,' Gabrielle heard him snarl. 'OK, shift!'

Deprived of sight, it was impossible to gauge the length of the trek across the gravel—maybe she walked thirty yards, maybe she walked fifty—but it ended in a climb up a flight of rickety, slippery and uneven wooden steps. Despite guidance her ascent was precarious, but behind her came the sound of Saul losing his footing, more blows and, among them, grunts of satisfaction. Gabrielle's stomach churned. The Scot was exhibiting sadistic tendencies.

'We're at the top,' said her escort. A door creaked and he guided her over a threshold. 'Hey presto!' he said, sounding like a magician, and removed the bag from her head.

Dazzled by the light, it took Gabrielle a moment or two to realise she was standing in the hallway of a small, compact and energetically furnished flat. Through a door on her right a king-sized bed dripped flounces of crimson and white satin and, as she walked forward, she glimpsed a bathroom, its walls covered with sketches of grottos and fountains and frolicking nymphs. The hall led into a square living area, and here the bedroom colour-scheme had been repeated. The walls were covered in dark red silk. A crimson chaise-longue and armchairs stood on a shaggy white carpet. The windows were hung with frilly crimson and white polka-dot curtains. Again on her right, a breakfast bar separated the living-room from a narrow strip of kitchen, and Gabrielle gawked at units and appliances, each dutifully painted crimson.

The sound of footsteps had her head whipping round to see Saul being roughly steered into the room. Like her, he was masked but, in addition, his hands had been tied in front of him. Her eyes widened in dismay. Earlier she had made a sarcastic reference to the two of them being bound, but now the twine which bit deep into his wrists shocked her to the core. Wrapped cruelly around, it was in danger of cutting off the blood. As the Scot appeared from behind him, Gabrielle instinctively drew back. With most of his features concealed, their captor had looked mean, but now he was exposed as a hostile and arrogant bully. The black hair shorn to a quarter-inch of his scalp, the pock-marked skin, the sneer which lifted one side of his fleshy mouth, seemed to have been specially designed to inspire fear.

'And who 'ave we 'ere?' he gibed.

He needed to lurch up in order to rip the bag away, but as he did her breath caught in horror. The skin above Saul's left eye was broken and bloody, his cheek had been bruised, and there were angry, swollen red weals to one side of his jaw. The blows she heard had been blows to the head and, from their severity, it was obvious the Scot had used the gun.

Gabrielle forgot all about being frightened. 'You swine!' she flared.

His accomplice, who had been revealed as a skinny, blond youth with a dumb grin, pushed a Christopher Robin fall of hair from his eyes. 'I'm not sure you should have done that, Jock,' he said. 'Mr Vincent didn't actually say what it is they've done, so suppose——'

'Wouldn't 'ave sent us to pick 'em up if they was his best buddies, would he? And even if he didn't tell us——' Jock tapped the side of a bulbous nose '—we know what they've been up to.'

'Which is?' Saul asked.

'I mind my own business, and if I was you I'd do the same,' his assailant rapped out. Still brandishing the gun, he took a penknife from his pocket with his free hand and, slashing recklessly, cut Saul's bindings. 'Come on, Phil,' he told the youth.

'You're going to fetch your boss?' Saul asked.

'Mr Vincent isn't the kind who gets *fetched*,' Jock sniggered. 'He'll be with you in his own good time.'

'But not today?' he hazarded, rubbing at his wrists.

'Not a chance.'

Gabrielle drew in an unsteady breath. Despite Saul's mention of a delay, somehow she had taken their prompt release for granted—and now she felt debilitated.

'You're—you're leaving us here overnight?' she asked weakly.

'No need to bust a gut.' Level with the bedroom, Jock leered inside. 'That bed's tailor-made for newly-weds.'

'Newly-weds?' she repeated.

'That was your big mistake.'

'How?' enquired Saul.

'Your weddin' photo appeared in the local paper, that's how Mr Vincent tracked you down. Not so smart as you thought, was you?' he taunted.

'IQ of ten,' Saul said pleasantly.

Jock frowned. His victims were not supposed to agree with him, they were supposed to squirm.

'Don't think you can escape,' he warned, needing to demonstrate his superiority. 'It's a thirty-foot drop from the window, and the door's solid. Even so, me and Phil'll be watching the stairs.'

'The two of you are SAS-trained?' Saul asked.

'Oh, no, we was never——' Realising his mistake, he scowled. 'We'll see yous in the morning.'

The moment the men had gone, Gabrielle rushed forward.

'Why did that—that *slimebag* need to beat you up?' she protested, anxiously inspecting his face.

He gave her a wry look. 'Don't tell me you're concerned about my welfare?'

'In my capacity as a paid-up member of the anti-violence league, yes! A cold compress might help. Stay there,' she ordered, and sped into the bathroom.

'You think I'm going somewhere?' Saul grinned, then winced. Grinning hurt.

'Sit down and put your head back.'

'There's nothing I enjoy more than a full-breasted young woman leaning over me,' Saul remarked, as she began pressing a tight-wrung flannel against his bumps and bruises. 'Ouch! Be gentle with me.'

'So sorry.'

'I bet,' he said wryly. 'I got walloped because I provoked the guy,' he explained. 'I wanted to have a look around, so when he put the bag over my head I pulled it off.'

'And were pistol-whipped for your pains.' Gabrielle shuddered. 'What did you see?'

'It was too dark to make out much, but we've

been brought to a large, rather impressive stone house in acres of parkland. Separate, and to one side, were buildings which looked like stables, stores, garages, that kind of thing. I figure we're in a granny-flat over one of them.'

'Must be a jazzy granny,' Gabrielle commented, her gaze flicking around the room.

'One with a crimson fetish,' he agreed.

She lifted the pad. 'Is this helping?'

Gingerly, Saul touched the graze above his eye. 'Yes. Thanks.'

His nose could have been broken, she thought, as she returned to her ministrations. Indeed, the way the Scot had obviously lashed out with the gun, Saul could have suffered brain damage or been blinded.

'Don't provoke Jock again,' she pleaded.

'No, ma'am.'

'I mean it, Saul. Whatever he does or wants you to do, just agree. Don't argue. Don't cross him. And don't make jokes he doesn't understand.'

'If the jerk tries to walk all over me, I'm to let him?' he protested.

'Yes!'

In the van she had felt relatively resilient, but now gloom and doom stalked all around.

'But that's exactly what he wants! Look, allowing someone of his mentality to gain the upper hand is the worst thing you can do.'

'I don't care. All I care about is——'

Saul fended off the compress and sat up. 'Are

you hungry?'

Gabrielle needed to think for a moment. 'A bit.'

'Then let's see if there's anything to eat.' In the kitchen, he opened cupboards and looked inside the fridge. 'You'll be pleased to hear Mr Vincent has no intention of allowing us to starve. There are the basics, like milk, bread, eggs, plus he's laid on enough freezer dinners to feed an army. There's even a couple of fresh trout.' Blue eyes met hers across the breakfast bar. 'You made us a wonderful *truites aux amandes* once. How about having a bash at something similar?'

Given their predicament, preparing a meal seemed a somewhat homespun and insubstantial activity, yet Gabrielle was forced to admit it was therapeutic. By the time she served grilled trout with basmati rice and frozen peas, her spirits had rallied.

'I feel almost human again,' she said, as they drank second cups of coffee. 'How about you?'

Saul risked a careful smile. 'Human, but bushwhacked—for want of a better term.'

'One way or another, you've had a traumatic day,' she sympathised, eyeing his injuries. 'I know it's very early, but why don't you have a shower and head for bed?'

'I'll shower, but as far as sleeping goes——' he nodded towards the chaise-longue where Gabrielle was sitting '—I'll use that.'

'You're the invalid, Saul, so the rules are you get

the bed.'

'I'm sleeping in here.'

'Wrong. I am.'

'Let's not argue.'

'Which of us has the greater need of a good night's sleep?' she enquired. 'You!' She patted the crimson velvet. 'Which is why I'm installing myself right here.'

Saul heaved a sigh. 'Don't make a five-act play out of this.'

'All you need to do is agree with me.'

'You never used to be so damn bossy!' he exploded.

'You never used to be so damn stubborn!'

It was impasse.

He wiped his hands on his thighs as he stood up. 'Why don't we both use the bed?' he suggested.

'Both?' Gabrielle echoed.

'If you're worried about me making advances, you needn't be,' Saul said crisply. 'Not only am I aware that the days when you and I created that marvellous mayhem are over, but the way I'm feeling I present as much of a threat to your womanhood as that eunuch you may, or may not, have been dating. Besides, if I did presume to lay just one finger on you, I know the damage you'd inflict would make Jock's battering fade into insignificance.'

Uneasily she chewed at her lip. 'I'm not sure it's a good idea,' she began.

'Gabby, lord knows how it happened, but we've been dropped into a situation where it seems sensible to keep our wits about us. Shouldn't we *both* try for a decent sleep?'

'I suppose so, but——'

'The bed must be six feet wide. There's plenty of room, dammit,' Saul rasped, his patience growing thin. 'If I sleep on top of the sheet and you go below, then nothing scandalous is going to happen—like me touching your naked flesh!'

Gabrielle flushed. 'OK.'

'Thank you,' he said laconically.

She rose and became busy clearing the table. 'While you're in the shower, I'll tidy up here,' she said, as she stacked plates. 'Then I'll have a bath.'

Saul raised a brow. 'A long one?'

'Could be,' Gabrielle agreed, wondering what he was getting at. 'I noticed a drier in the bathroom, so I thought I'd also shampoo my hair. And blow-drying it afterwards will take time,' she explained.

'Delaying the evil moment?' he suggested, and her cheeks burned even pinker. 'You needn't bother. I guarantee that if you come to bed more than one minute after me, I shall be fast asleep.'

He was.

CHAPTER SIX

ON FIRST slipping oh, so stealthily into bed, Gabrielle had been wary. With eyes closed, one arm curled across the top of his head, and his breathing rhythmic, Saul looked dead to the world—but for how long? In an hour or two, would he wake up, roll over and draw her close? His curt dismissal of Dana Kelham indicated the relationship had sailed into troubled waters, albeit temporarily, so loyalty there would not prove a problem—and Saul always had possessed a strong sexual drive.

If he did wrap his arms around her, what then? Gabrielle's heart began to vibrate. He had prophesied that the least advance would have her scratching and biting and fighting him off, yet regrettably she could not share his conviction. Over the past year—well, two—out of the blue and for no apparent reason she had been hit by bolts of tingling, zinging, physical desire. At such times, she had yearned to run her hands over a broad bare back. She had craved masculine strength, masculine power, masculine drive. She had ached for the abandonment and relief of lovemaking. The longing passed—a swift immersion into business invariably proved diverting—yet each time it left her feeling restless and increasingly susceptible. Gazing at the strong lines of his profile, at the gleam of his golden shoulders, Gabrielle sighed. Whatever else she felt about him, she could not deny that Saul O'Connor was a lethally attractive man.

She switched off the bedside-lamp and turned away on to her side. Unlike him, she would not plunge into instant slumber. The jitters would keep her awake. Jitters allied to Saul. Jitters concerning the unlikely events of the day. Jitters about their daunting situation. She would never sleep.

Gabrielle yawned and rubbed her eyes. In her comatose state she was unsure of her surroundings, and for a bleary moment she struggled to place herself, then she snapped awake. For the first time in her life she had, she realised, spent a night in captivity—and a look at her watch revealed it had been nine hours of solid rest. Also, for the first time in years, she had spent the night with a man! Hastily her eyes slide sideways and, to her relief, she saw that the space beside her was empty. The man in question had already risen.

'Sleep well?' Saul enquired, coming in a minute or two later. Dressed, and with his dark hair brushed, he was returning from the bathroom.

'Yes, amazingly.' She peered at him over the bedspread's extravagant flounces. 'How's the face?'

'I managed to shave,' he said, in blithe dismissal

of the deep purple bruises on his jaw and his
scarred brow.

Gabrielle frowned. 'What time do you think Mr
Vincent's likely to appear?' she fretted.

'I don't know, and until we've had our breakfast
I don't intend to bother about him.'

'Not bother?' she squeaked.

'Not yet. Gabby, it's what's called getting your
priorities straight.'

She thought about that. 'What can you see from
the window?' she asked.

'Nothing of any significance. It overlooks a
flagged quadrangle lined with stables and
garages.'

'There was no glimpse of the outside world?'

'None. The view's very restricted.'

'Were there any signs of life?'

'Like a guy stalking around with ''Vincent''
tattooed on his forehead?' Saul enquired
pungently, then he relented. 'I saw no one. All the
doors were closed and the place seems deserted.
There wasn't even a clue as to where Jock and
partner might be based. He reckoned they would
be watching the stairs, but there hasn't been a
sound from them so I suspect they could be much
further away.'

'It is quiet,' Gabrielle agreed.

'Are you planning to stay there all day, or is it
my presence which is stopping you from getting out
of bed?' he enquired, as she continued to lie there.
He hooked his thumbs in the hip pockets of his
jeans and grinned, solidly remaining *in situ*. 'It

seems strange that a woman who demonstrates such *chutzpah* in business, and who once took considerable pleasure in displaying herself before me, should now be so fraught with inhibitions.'

She flung back the sheet. 'I'm not inhibited.'

'Inhibited and incredibly prissy,' Saul stated, as she stood up. 'I assumed you'd gone to bed naked, but here you are——' he arched a sardonic brow '——Little Miss Demure in her bra and pants.'

Gabrielle did not feel demure. Anything but. Her black lace underwear was of the fashionably minimal variety, and with the swell of her breasts and the creamy curve of her thighs exposed to his gaze she felt disturbingly wanton. There was something in the way his eyes lingered which belied the 'demure' label, too.

'I'm surprised you didn't wear your sweatshirt and tights, with a chastity belt topping the lot,' he went on. 'Ah, I forgot, your sweatshirt's dirty——'

'Filthy. I wonder if there's anything I could wear in here,' she said, and marched past him to yank open the doors of a white louvred wardrobe. 'Wow!' she exclaimed, while Saul gave a low whistle.

A long rail was packed tight with satin hangers bearing women's clothes—many bright-coloured, many shot through with metallic thread, and all of the 'Hollywood starlet' type. Raking through, Gabrielle found diaphanous dresses, back-baring blouses, a pair of white plastic trousers which laced up the sides. When she reached a scarlet bustier trimmed with silver ribbons, Saul groaned.

'Wear that and—tie me to a stake if this is not the truth—you'll make all my fantasies come alive.'

Refusing—impolitely—Gabrielle continued looking until she came to a black angora sweater. The boat-shaped neck swooped lower than she would have liked, but it was one of the less flamboyant items. To accompany it, she chose a black suede mini-skirt trimmed with silver studs. Again this was not ideal but, unlike most of the clothes which were too big, it was her size. Below the rail, shoes had been neatly arranged. There were mules lavish with tulle roses, gold lamé stilettos, sandals fashioned from thin chains.

'These look fun,' she said, trying on a pair of shortie black satin boots. 'And they fit.'

From a shelf she purloined a packet of tights and, armed with her spoils, she went off to the bathroom.

When she emerged, Saul was sitting at the breakfast bar where he had toast and coffee waiting.

'If you're thinking of appearing on television dressed like that, the authorities'll need to issue an "adults only" warning,' he grinned, his eyes absorbing the flirty neckline, the brief, hip-hugging skirt, her fishnetted legs. 'You're definitely X-rated.'

Gabrielle pulled a face. 'At least what I'm

wearing is clean.'

'This whole place is clean, and well-equipped,'
he said, dragging his eyes from her to look around.
'There's everything from pots and pans to
disposable razors to——'

'Useless cutlery,' she sighed, waving her knife.
Like all the knives and forks, it was made of cheap
white bendy plastic.

'Mr Vincent mustn't want us to cut
ourselves—or his henchmen,' Saul remarked
drily.

'Or the toast!' She sawed in desperation. 'I pity
the regular occupants if they have to struggle like
this.'

'But are there regular occupants? I'd say the flat
hasn't been used recently, and may never have been
permanently lived in at all.'

'You could be right,' she agreed. 'Everything
does seem relatively untouched. I wonder who
comes here, and why? I wonder who chose the
horrendous colour-scheme, and who owns the
clothes. I wonder——' Gabrielle stopped short.
Feet were clattering up the outside stairs. 'Oh,
heavens,' she said, in alarm.

'We sit here and finish our breakfast.' Saul
placed his hand over hers. 'And whatever happens,
we don't let the bastards grind us down—OK?'

She spot-welded on a smile. 'OK.'

Jock was first into the room. Swaggering and
flaunting the gun, his appearance had not been
improved by daylight. In crumpled tracksuit,
which looked as though it had been slept in, and

with dark stubble covering his chin, he made an unkempt and menacing figure. Following in his wake came Phil, who seemed ill at ease and very much second-string.

Saul nodded a greeting. 'Good morning. Would you care to join us for a cup of coffee?'

The cordial invitation rocked the Scot back on his heels, and for a moment his mouth worked silently. 'Coffee?' he got out at last, as though he had been invited to drink cyanide.

'Mr Vincent doesn't appear to be with you, so I thought you might fancy some while we're waiting.'

Jock recovered his equilibrium. 'You've got your timing wrong, big boy,' he sneered, his lip twisting. 'You'll get through a lot more than one cup of coffee before—hey, what do you think you're wearing?' he demanded, suddenly noticing Gabrielle. The black eyes bulged. 'Them's not your clothes.'

She remembered how yesterday she had begged Saul not to rile the brute—and Saul's response. And she thought of his encouragement today.

'Don't you approve?' she enquired, calmly biting into her toast.

'No bloody way!'

'Neither would Babs if she knew,' Phil said, with a giggle. 'She'd be furious. Fussy about her things is Babs. Must have everything just so. And houseproud? I thought my mum——'

'Take off that jumper!' Jock blasted, looking ready to rip the clothes from her himself. 'And the skirt. And them boots.'

'Take it easy,' Saul said quietly.

'I'll change if, and when, Mr Vincent asks me to change,' Gabrielle declared. Saul had kept hold of her hand, and she hooked her little finger around his, gripping tight. 'Rush me into taking anything off now, and——' she faked a smile '—sorry, I could tear it.'

The Scot glowered. He had been outmanoeuvred and he did not like it. 'You're going to be waiting quite a while for Mr Vincent,' he said, determined to prick their composure. These two customers were far too cool. 'I've just been through to 'im, and it seems some business matter's cropped up, so he won't be able to get over here until later in the week.'

'When, later in the week?' Saul enquired.

'Maybe not until Friday.'

Gabrielle slid down from her stool. 'We could be here for another four days?' she said dully.

'Shame, ain't it?' Jock sniggered, now able to indulge in some heavy-duty gloating. 'Not nice just hanging around, waiting for the boss to arrive. Not much fun twiddling your thumbs and wondering what he's goin' to——'

Saul's tongue moistened his lips. 'I have a confession to make,' he interrupted. 'Back in Kensington I gave you the impression we were Mr and Mrs Arnott, but we aren't.' He glanced quickly at Gabrielle. 'My name is Saul O'Connor.' He paused. 'And this is Gabrielle Peters. We've never heard of your Mr Vincent and——'

'You know nothing about two kilos of cocaine which 'ave gone walkies either, I suppose?' Jock interrupted. 'Cocaine which was Mr Vincent's property until you two did a bunk.'

'Cocaine?' Gabrielle said, in astonishment.

'No, we don't. Drugs are not our scene,' Saul replied. 'I'm a businessman and strictly legit.'

'And I have some shops,' she put in. She looked for a narrowing of eyes, a glimmer of recognition, but neither man showed any response. Gabrielle Peters, shop owner, was not so famous, after all. She held out her hand to Phil. 'If I was Mrs Arnott and newly married, I'd be wearing engagement and wedding rings, wouldn't I? Look, I have neither.'

As the youth surveyed her fingers, his brow furrowed. 'But why say you were the Arnotts if you aren't?'

'She didn't. I did,' Saul inserted. 'At the time I had some cock-eyed idea about it being safer to go along with you and let Mr Vincent discover the mistake.'

The Scot moved forward, jostling Phil aside. 'And now you have some cock-eyed idea that you can persuade us to believe all this—well, we don't! We don't believe a word!' Stubby fingers adjusted their grip on the gun which pointed in Saul's direction. 'Shame the boss can't get over to see you earlier, isn't it?' he said, greedy to wallow in their discomfort again.

'Get over from where?' Saul enquired.

'From——' Jock thought better of telling them.

'I trust you're not complainin',' he taunted. 'Babs wasn't pleased when Mr Vincent told her someone would be staying here, and at such short notice, but this little palace is perfect.'

'Apart from the leak in the bathroom,' Saul said.

'Leak? What leak?' Jock asked sharply.

'There's a drip at the back of the washbasin. It's wetting the carpet.'

'Crikey, Babs'll throw a fit!' Phil exclaimed, casting his partner an anxious look. 'Suppose she complains to Mr Vincent and he blames us? He did say to keep an eye out for things, and y'know what happens if you get on the wrong side of 'im.' The youth tugged fretfully at his fringe. 'Do you think I ought to have a shot at mending it?'

'How much of a leak is it?' Jock demanded.

'Minor at the moment, though obviously it'll get worse if it doesn't receive attention. Want me to show you where it is?' Saul suggested.

Phil gave a nod. 'Please.'

'No, you don't!' the Scot snarled abruptly. 'I've tumbled to your game, big boy. A leak—fat chance! What you intend to do is get the lad alone, then knock him out. Nice try, but——' he jabbed a triumphant thumb into his chest '—yours truly wasn't born yesterday.'

Saul shrugged. 'If you prefer the pipe to drip, that's up to you. But the carpet's going to be ruined.'

Uncertainty wrote itself large on the older man's face. For agonised moments, he floundered back and forth, visibly attempting to reach a decision, until finally he swung the gun from Saul and jerked it towards Gabrielle.

'You show Phil,' he instructed.

Her agreement was serene, yet inside she quaked. Had Saul told the truth? Gabrielle wondered, as she led the way towards the bathroom. She had not noticed any damp, so his talk of seepage could be a trick—and, if it was, Jock would be sure to take the deception as a personal insult and react violently. Thoughts of the atrocities the bully could commit sent a shiver quivering down her spine. She must do something, but what? Could she dip her hand into the basin and somehow moisten the pipe? Gabrielle wondered. Could she leap forward, spin on the taps and splash water all over the place? But, before she had a chance to do anything, Phil pushed past her into the bathroom and dropped down beside the basin.

'Behind here, is it?' he asked.

'I—I think so,' she croaked.

The youth tipped his head and frowned up. He studied the pipework for a long, silent moment and then, with a curse, he clambered to his feet.

'Is something wrong?' she asked, her heart in her mouth.

'Yes,' he grumbled, and showed her circles of wet on the knees of his jeans.

Gabrielle laughed, and handed him a towel. 'You can kneel on this. Babs has some very glamorous clothes,' she remarked, as he loosened the carpet from the edging strip and rolled it carefully back from the basin.

'Babs is one glamorous gal. Long blonde hair. Mouth-watering figure. The sexiest wiggle you ever did see.' Phil looked up and grinned. 'Though most women seem to wiggle when they wear tight skirts,' he said pointedly. 'Trust old Vincent to grab himself the cream of the crop,' he continued. 'Mind you, Babs doesn't come cheap. She insisted he buy her a penthouse in the Docklands development, and when it came to setting her up with this little love-nest, no expense was spared.'

'Babs is Mr Vincent's mistress?'

'And how!' he chuckled. 'Nothing low profile about that affair, thanks to Babs. Everyone knows about her, even his wife.'

'*I* don't know about her. I've never heard of the woman,' Gabrielle said quickly. 'And, presumably, if I was Rita Arnott I would?'

The youth frowned. 'Maybe.'

'Doesn't Mr Vincent's wife mind about Babs?' she asked, content to have planted another seed of doubt.

'She's furious, but her hubbie isn't the kind you argue with. I understand she was real cheesed off when he had this place fixed up for Babs. Bit of a cheek, bringing another woman in right beside her in the big house.'

'I'd call it a lot of a cheek!'

Phil laughed. 'Yeah. Only someone like the boss could get away with it. But his wife's hardly ever there. Prefers the sunshine on the Costa del Sol, she does.' He wedged his arm behind the pipes and prodded, then sat back. 'The joint needs tightening. It's a simple job. Just take a minute with the right tools.'

In the living-room he explained the problem to Jock, and after a discussion it was agreed they would locate a wrench.

'See you later,' the Scot sniggered. 'And as you'll be here quite a while, please make yourselves at home.'

'Will do,' Saul said calmly.

'Friday!' Gabrielle wailed, the moment they were alone. As the door closed, so her brave front had evaporated. Despondently, she dropped down on to the chaise-longue. 'I imagined we'd be back home today, instead of which——'

'What did Phil have to say?' he cut in.

'Sorry?'

'You were talking to him. At length.'

Saul was so insistent on knowing what had been said that Gabrielle had no alternative but to stash her thoughts to one side and relay the conversation.

'Sounds like this Vincent guy could be in Spain, too,' he mused, when she had finished.

'Spain?' Her worries plunged into fresh soil, took instant root, rampaged like jungle vines. 'Suppose his business drags on? Suppose he can't get back to England? Oh, no!' Her hand flew to her throat and she gazed at him in horror. 'Suppose he decides to ship us out there?'

'What as—"his and hers" white slaves? You've been watching too much television.'

Gabrielle leapt up to peer out of the window. 'Jock was right, it is a long way down.' She rushed to the door and gave the handle a twist and a desperate two-handed tug. 'He told the truth about this, too.'

'If only I hadn't flunked that course in lock-picking,' Saul murmured.

'Now we know why there's so much food.' In her agitation, the sweater had slipped to reveal a bare shoulder, and she hoisted it back. 'There must be enough to last for weeks, if not months. Months—oh, heavens! If Mr Vincent puts fear and trembling into everybody, even Jock,' Gabrielle continued, wildly jumping track, 'then he must be a real hard individual. Ruthless. One who stops at nothing.' She grabbed hold of his sleeve. 'Saul, we've got to get out of here. We must! If drugs are involved, this is big crime.'

'You don't need to tell me how serious the situation is; I know.'

'What are we going to do? When Mr Vincent sees we aren't the Arnotts, maybe he won't free us. Maybe he'll decide it would be simpler to——' her voice fell to a hoarse whisper and she looked at him aghast '—to eliminate us.'

'I love it when you talk stupid,' Saul said impatiently.

'Stupid? I don't consider——'

He jabbed a finger at her. 'Shut up, sit down and listen.'

'I don't——' Gabrielle began again, but the searing blue of his eyes silenced her and she did as instructed.

'I know you're scared, I know you feel panicky, and I sympathise. Hell, I'm not having a knees-up myself! But if you start imagining hazards, then you'll dig yourself a hole which you can't climb out of,' he decreed. 'What we must do is look at the facts. For a start, our situation could be worse. True, it could be better but, whatever you say, being dumped in this place is light years away from being assigned a cell in Death Row.'

Gabrielle lowered her head. 'I guess so,' she muttered.

'However, I agree with your character-reading of Vincent, and I think it would be unwise to hang around here until he shows up, if not reckless in the extreme.'

'You reckon we should try to escape?'

'Escape, or persuade our captors to let us go. So, on to fact two—Jock and Phil are not the brightest of mortals. Indeed, Jock is a concrete man with a cement mentality. Whereas—fact three—you are a clever girl and, unlikely though it may seem at times, my speciality is formulating intelligent manoeuvres. Between us we should be able to outwit them,' Saul insisted. 'We should be able to come up with *something*.'

Gabrielle frowned, thinking. 'There are two ways to escape,' she said slowly. 'Either we overpower them and make a dash for it, or we find some way of getting out of here on the sly.' She bit her lip. 'Attempting to overpower them——'

'Is too dangerous,' Saul rejected, before she could get any further. 'If we're going to break out, then we must inspect the flat and try to find a trap-door, loose floorboards, a false wall—some point of weakness. As soon as they've been back and fixed the leak, we'll make a start.' He hesitated. 'I hope you didn't mind me taking the initiative and giving them our real names? The delay with Vincent changed the entire ballgame, and pretending to be someone else *is* complicated and it could rebound.'

'I'm glad you told them,' Gabrielle assured him. 'I don't suppose you're carrying any kind of identity?' she enquired after a moment. 'Your name on a credit card, an initial on a handkerchief—something like that?'

Saul emptied his pockets. ''Fraid not,' he said, frowning at a car-key and a handful of loose change. 'I suddenly decided I had to see you, so I jumped in the car and——'

'I thought you said you were in my neighbourhood?'

'I lied. Have you got any ID?'

'None.' The way Saul had spoken made it plain his visit had derived from a personal rather than a business motive and, although she was not exactly sure why it should, Gabrielle found this intensely pleasing. It was all she could do not to smile. 'Never mind,' she continued, 'despite Jock's insistence, Phil has his doubts about us being the Arnotts—so a few more prods could work wonders.'

Saul lifted a brow. 'You've stopped singing the jailhouse blues?' he enquired drily.

'Yes.' Now she did smile. 'I'm sorry I became paranoid. It's not like me to get so wired up.'

'We all have our flip side.'

'You're not saying you crack at times, too?' she protested.

He grinned. 'I do. It's just that it's harder to recognise because——' He stopped. 'The dastardly duo have returned.'

When the door opened Jock marched into the living-room to take up sentry duty, while his companion carried a tool-box into the bathroom.

'Shall I see if Phil needs help?' Gabrielle enquired, keen to start her persuasive sales talk.

'You stay right there,' the Scot growled.

She was wondering whether she should argue, if she dared argue, when the youth reappeared. His diagnosis had been correct. The job had taken only a minute.

'Success!' he grinned.

'Good lad,' Jock muttered, in rare praise. 'Let's get out of here.'

Saul stepped forward. 'I'm staying in Suite 121 at the Elliott Tower Hotel. Give them a ring and ask if they have a guest by the name of Saul O'Connor, when I was last there, and what I look like. One phone call, that's all it needs.'

'And all you need is to know of this O'Connor bloke, who happens to be tall and dark-haired like you!' Jock sneered.

'But how could I have arranged for him to disappear?' Saul demanded angrily. 'I couldn't. It's impossible!'

A bulldozer jaw set solid. 'We're not ringing no hotels.'

'To check my identity, go to my house and look through my papers,' Gabrielle appealed. 'As Mr Vincent isn't coming for a day or two, you have plenty of time.'

Phil shot Jock a wary look. 'We could. And we could phone——'

'These are all tricks,' his partner declared.

'Like the leak?' Saul enquired.

The Scot scrubbed at the end of his nose. 'What big boy wants,' he informed the youth, 'is for one of us to drive off and leave the other alone. Then he makes his move. He gets you or me up here, and rushes us.'

'For heaven's sake, man!' Saul grated. 'I'm not going to rush someone who's carrying a gun.'

'You might.'

His mouth tightened in exasperation. 'OK, before anyone leaves you can tie me up.'

'No one's leaving.'

'You can tie me up, too,' Gabrielle offered.

'I'll bloody well tie up the both of you if you don't shut yer mouths!' the Scot shouted. 'Me and Phil aren't going nowhere, and we're not making no phone calls, and that's that.'

'The next time you speak to Mr Vincent, ask him what the Arnotts look like,' Saul instructed.

'I'm not asking 'im nothing!'

Saul sighed. 'Whatever Mr Vincent is paying, I'll increase it if you let us go,' he said, after a moment of silence.

'Increase it to what?' Phil enquired.

'Name your figure. I'm open to negotiation.'

The youth sidled alongside Jock. 'Old Vincent's not being that generous,' he mumbled, out of the corner of his mouth.

'No!'

'Suppose I treble the cash?' Saul suggested. 'That way you'll not only avoid being shown up as incompetent, you'll also be quids in.'

'No!'

'You don't need the two of us, so keep me here and let Gabby go,' he appealed. 'Tell me how much you want to free her, and I'll pay it.'

'You mustn't, Saul!' she protested, in alarm. 'I'm not leaving you here on your own.'

'A thousand pounds, will that do?'

Phil gazed at him slack-jawed. 'A thousand?' he repeated incredulously.

Jock grabbed hold of the youth's arm and bundled him into the hallway.

'I said no big boy!' he barked, and the door slammed shut.

'If he calls you "big boy" once more, I shall strangle him with his own epiglottis!' Gabrielle flared, but Saul was preoccupied with his own thoughts.

'Next time they visit, I'll up the ante,' he decided.

'To secure my release?' Her eyes flashed. 'Don't you dare!'

He rubbed a hand wearily across his face. 'Gabby, this whole situation is my fault, and I shall do my damnedest to get you out of here.'

'No!'

'Hell, don't you start.'

'The situation is not your fault,' Gabrielle insisted. 'Look further back, and it's clear it's me who's to blame.'

'Because of the burglar alarm? But anyone can forget——'

'Not the alarm. You see, as you said something without thinking it through, so I bought the house in the same way. From the start Kevin maintained the Arnotts were fishy characters. He couldn't understand why they should be in such a hurry and so eager for spot cash. He said I must try to find out who they were, what their background was, and warned me not to become involved until I'd satisfied myself they had a legitimate reason for their departure, but I didn't. I signed the papers within days.' Gabrielle sighed. 'And now it's obvious they suspected Mr Vincent had discovered their whereabouts.'

Saul sprawled in an armchair, one leg flung over the arm. 'In the heat of the moment, it's easy to think you're doing the right thing when, in fact, you're making a major mistake,' he said ruefully.

As she looked across at where he sat, a wave of nostalgia swept over her. He had often sat like that in the past, she remembered. And they had often chatted. And in the past, too, there had been a time of intense pressure, as they were under pressure now. Then her emotions had bubbled up like Vesuvius and spilled out in hot and ill-considered coals, but today she had held on to her composure. Today she was on top of the situation, rather than the situation being on top of her—and it was all thanks to Saul.

'I—I committed a major mistake once before,' Gabrielle ventured, in a low, thoughtful voice.

'And we both know what that was,' he said brusquely. 'You agreeing to move in with me.' Saul rose to his feet. 'Let's start our inspection of the flat, shall we?'

CHAPTER SEVEN

CONSTANTLY vigilant for sounds of their captors' return, they embarked on a painstaking examination of the flat. Walls were tapped, floors paced and prodded, the insides of cupboards scrutinised, but not one weak spot was discovered. Their prison seemed impregnable. Even extravagant ideas of either breaking or removing the living-room window and shinnying down on sheets had to be discarded, because the window was an impenetrable sealed double-glazed unit.

'The only thing for it is to create our own exit point,' Saul said, with a sigh.

'How?' Gabrielle looked around. 'Where?'

'The carpet's already been disturbed in the bathroom, so let's roll it back further and try to prise up a floorboard. Who knows, there might be an open drop beneath.' He rubbed at his jaw. 'The problem is, what the hell do we use for prising?'

'How about the hook of a coat hanger?'

'Did I say this kid was clever?' he asked an invisible audience. 'She's a genius!'

As Saul tried to force the wire down between the

planking, she took up guard duty by the door. He poked, the wire buckled, he straightened it and poked again. And again. And again. The floor was new and tightly constructed; the removal of a board threatened to be a long, difficult job. She looked at her watch. Monday midday, and tycoon Saul O'Connor was waging war on a piece of wood while the busy-busy Gabrielle Peters watched—how unusual, she thought whimsically. If only someone had missed them. If only someone had raised the alarm. The likelihood of the police tracking them down seemed remote, yet to know a search had been instigated would be some reason for hope.

'Are you *sure* Dana Kelham won't try to make contact?' Gabrielle asked.

'Positive.'

'But even if the two of you have quarrelled, she could decide you're not such a bad guy, after all, and——'

Saul glanced up. 'You've got it wrong. Until a few days ago I'd never even seen the woman on television, let alone met her in person. Then, out of the blue, she rang to say her department was planning a series on what makes today's businessman tick, and they wanted to include me,' he explained. 'I told her I was sorry, but I didn't have the time—nor the inclination. Baring my soul, and my teeth, for a TV camera does not appeal,' he inserted, as an aside. 'However, she said a guy I've known since school had given her my name, and could I at least listen? Out of courtesy to my friend, and because the woman was so damned insistent, I agreed to meet her for dinner.' Half the hook was embedded. Cautiously he turned it, tugged, and muttered an expletive as it shot straight out again. 'She began by making what appeared to be innocent enquiries about my first job, the one with White Group,' he said, as he prodded the hook between the floorboards again, 'but swiftly moved on to searching questions about Robert White's relationship with my uncle.'

Gabrielle's brows drew together. She had not known there was a relationship, as such. 'Why should that interest Dana Kelham?' she asked.

'Because they detest each other.'

'Do they?' she said, in surprise.

'Yes. Thirty years ago they entered into a joint venture, but somewhere along the way the deal went sour. My uncle won't talk about it—to me, to anyone—but legend has it there were errors on both sides. Whatever, neither of them would accept any blame and each accused the other of malpractice. There was massive bad feeling at the time, threats of court cases, and over the years the acrimony has festered.' He broke off to pay concerted attention to the hook, then continued, 'Robert White and my uncle are both proud and essentially private men who would hate to have their dirty linen washed in public, so the feud's been kept a secret, particularly from the media. But if they find themselves in the same club, the same restaurant, attending the same business meeting, one immediately leaves.'

Gabrielle's mind went back. 'Then Sir Jeffrey didn't fix your job with the White Group?'

'Hell, no! Like many other big companies, Whites brought a team along to the university and interviewed people for various vacancies which existed within the group. I applied for one, and was accepted.' Saul grinned. 'When I told my uncle I'd be working for his arch enemy, he damn near tore me apart. But I'd made my choice.'

She listened for noises, but all was quiet. 'How did Robert White react?' she asked curiously.

'He was the big wheel while I was a very small cog, so it took ages before he realised exactly whom his personnel department had hired. However, by that time I'd begun to prove my worth, so——' His shrug was more eloquent than a soliloquy.

'And Dana Kelham had found about the feud and hoped to reveal it on television?'

Saul nodded. 'Her idea was to zap the business world with an exclusive disclosure and, although she didn't admit it in so many words, create as much trouble as possible. Yet despite having ferreted out a number of rumours, she lacked facts. That evening over dinner the woman did her damnedest to induce me to share confidences, even to the extent of suggesting——' the harshness of his tone denoted his disgust '—I might care to share her bed.'

Gabrielle's brows rose. So *he* had been the—attempted—seduced and not the seducer? She owed him an apology.

'Tacky,' she said.

'Isn't it? But, believe me, there's a breed of single-minded females stalking this earth who are prepared to do anything to get what they want.'

Although she murmured a comment about how hardboiled the television reporter must be, Gabrielle could not help thinking that perhaps Dana Kelham had not been entirely single-minded. Saul packed more virility into his little finger than most men had in their entire bodies, and sleeping with him hardly ranked as a fate worse than death. Indeed, considering how unaware of his own attractions he had always been in the past, it could be a case of him interpreting Dana Kelham's wants the wrong way round!

'But the loyal nephew rejected all her advances?' Gabrielle enquired, her dimples deepening.

'She was shaped like an ironing-board,' Saul replied, looking up at her to grin. 'Not my type. I prefer women with curves.' As if in confirmation, his blue gaze travelled up her legs, over her hips, to rest on the soft surge of her breasts beneath the black angora. He frowned, then bent back to his task. 'But in any case, I practise safe sex now, which means cold showers and long conversations—like this one,' he muttered, thumping a fist against the recalcitrant hanger. 'Over the next couple of days, Dana Kelham bombarded me with phone calls demanding to be given my opinion on the feud,' he continued, 'but I refused to comment. Always politely, because I had a suspicion she could be recording our conversations in the hope of me losing my temper, and then she'd incorporate the tape in her programme as some kind of evidence. When the calls kept coming I contacted my friend and asked if he would kindly whistle in this persecutor he'd foisted on me, but it turned out the guy didn't know her.'

'Then he hadn't passed on your name?'

'No way. She must have felt she needed an "in" to me, so she'd made one up.'

'The sneaky so-and-so!' Gabrielle exclaimed.

'Conniving bitch,' he corrected. 'The next time Miss Kelham telephoned, I advised her that I knew of the deception, I was sick of her harassment, and warned that if she rang me again I would be complaining in the strongest terms to her chairman. It was the last call.'

Once more, the wire was in position between the boards. Once more Saul attempted to find purchase and, once more, he failed.

'Shall I have a try?' Gabrielle suggested.

Tiredly, he gave her the hanger. 'Be my guest.'

For ten minutes, she pushed and eased and thumped.

'Let's have something to eat,' he suggested, when she sat back on her heels and sighed. 'A break will do us good.'

In the kitchen, she examined the contents of the larder. 'You used to like tomato soup,' Gabrielle recalled, grinning back over her shoulder.

'I still do. And you?'

'And me.'

'I know you said no one at the office is going to miss you this week, but how about your friends?' Saul enquired, as he took the can from her to open it.

Gabrielle frowned, trying to think of someone who might attempt to get in touch. 'I don't have many friends outside work,' she confessed, when names stubbornly refused to appear. 'I'm so plumbed into Anniversaries that most people have given up on me. You can't blame them.' She poured the soup into a pan, placed the pan on the hob, took a sliced loaf from the bread bin. 'In fact,' she said, in awakening consternation, 'apart from my parents, I'm not close to *anyone* outside Anniversaries.'

'It's not the end of the world,' Saul protested, as she gazed at him with horrified green eyes.

'It must be pretty damn close! And most of the

people I see a lot of at work can't really be classed as friends; they're more acquaintances.'

Downcast and concerned, Gabrielle stirred the soup. Once there had always been someone with whom she could giggle, or divest herself of troubles. Yet somehow she had reached the state where her social contact was a flicker away from nil.

'But this is a situation which can be rectified,' Saul insisted. 'Yes?'

She straightened. 'Yes,' she agreed.

He slid his hands into his hip pockets and leant back against the breakfast bar, the denim stretched tight across his thighs. 'You were always full of original ideas when it came to selecting gifts—you gave me a book of poetry once which, much to my surprise, I enjoyed, and which I still have—is that what prompted you to start Anniversaries?'

Gabrielle nodded. 'Everyone reckoned I had a flair for the unusual, and it seemed like a talent I might be able to market.'

'Tell me about your shops,' he said. 'Start with the first one and give me a blow-by-blow account all the way up to twelve.'

'That would take ages!' she protested.

He moved broad shoulders. 'We've plenty of time.'

Her dialogue began reluctantly, but soon she gained enthusiasm. Saul had always been a good listener and, with his encouragement, tales of trials and tribulations, long-forgotten moments of joy, snippets of black humour, began tumbling out. Gabrielle talked through lunch, but his interruptions slowed her advance and when they returned to the bathroom her second shop had yet to be mentioned. As the afternoon passed, and they poked and prodded at the floorboard in turns, she relived her scramble up the ladder of success. She had reached shop eight when Saul achieved the first significant splintering of wood, an achievement which had them smiling at each other like delirious loons. It might not be cause for great celebration, yet it was a comforting start. Progress was being made. Evening came and they stopped for lasagne, which was eaten to the accompaniment of shops eleven and twelve.

'There must be a considerable number of young women whose sole aim is to emulate Gabrielle Peters!' said Saul, when she reached the end of her recital.

'Maybe,' she agreed lightly, yet as they resumed the attack on their escape route Gabrielle acknowledged that she represented a role-model only for dyed-in-the-wool careerists. A short time ago she would have taken this as a compliment, but wasn't a careerist someone who valued the success of her career above all else? Did she? If she had a shop every fifty yards and no friends for miles, would she be happy? Her work absorbed and excited her, yet so would so many other things in life—if she gave them half a chance.

She heaved a sigh. The prospect of never again abandoning herself to the spontaneous pleasures he had mentioned seemed unbearably grim.

'Now it's your turn to tell all,' she said, performing a mental veer. 'Start with—hold on.' Gabrielle poked her head out of the bathroom door, and grimaced. 'Guess who are back.'

The carpet was replaced, the hanger slung on the rail, and when Jock and Phil entered Gabrielle and Saul were sitting nonchalantly on the chaise-longue. There was a tense moment when the youth visited the bathroom to check on his repair—would he discover their clandestine activities?—but he came out beaming. Their attempt at conversation, in the hope of more persuasion, was cut short by Jock, who ordered a swift departure. The Scot was not going to have anyone filling *him* with troublesome doubts. Alone once more, they spent the remainder of the evening easing what had proved to be a stubbornly resistant floorboard, while Saul described his early progress.

At eleven o'clock, they decided to call a halt. They had not achieved much, but enough was enough and, 'To pile on the clichés,' as Saul remarked, 'tomorrow is another day.' The previous sleeping-arrangement had, admittedly, worked well and, although Gabrielle felt far from casual about sharing a bed again, because he appeared to take the routine for granted she kept quiet. OK, she did not feel casual, but what *did* she feel? Again, when she crept in beside him, Saul was fast asleep. Wary the first night, now irritation held sway. He was lying on his side facing away from her, and she scowled at the back of his head. He could have stayed awake long enough to say goodnight! she thought peevishly. It would have been polite. And, after a day when he had held her hand, and told her that he had *had* to see her, and made it plain how much he admired her shape, he could have—— Could have what? Wrenching the sheet around her, Gabrielle turned to glare through the darkness at the opposite wall. It was not as though she desired any kind of sexual approach, it was just that—that his instant sleep was hardly flattering!

Despite her irritation, again Gabrielle slept well, and when she awoke the next day she felt surprisingly buoyant—for someone who had spent her second night under lock and key!

After breakfast they commenced battle with the floorboard once more and, with a break to accommodate a terse check-up from Jock and Phil, Saul continued his narrative. Like hers, his career had been rich with incident and, because he was so amusing and sent her off into side-tracking laughter, the story took time. It was mid-afternoon before he completed describing his final job in the States.

'When you mention California, everyone

imagines it's a playground where you do nothing but lie on the beaches and get a tan all day,' he said, nudging the hook of the hanger more firmly into place. 'They're wrong. Everyone works damned hard. It's the survival of the fittest out there.'

'And to keep in trim you chewed up the tennis court each day at dawn?'

'Untrue.'

'Is it?' Gabrielle said, surprised.

'Completely.' Saul grinned. 'Though if I ever meet whichever reporter was responsible for spreading that little fabrication, I shall go down on my knees. The guy's done wonders for my reputation.'

'You didn't play tennis?'

'Yes, in the evenings and at the weekends. I also surf-boarded, did some big-game fishing, and went to wonderful barbecues.'

Gabrielle gave a wistful smile. 'Must have been fun.'

'It was.'

She tipped her head to one side. 'You had girlfriends?'

'One or two. Nothing serious,' he said dismissively. 'There were a number of "singles" in the complex where I lived, and we tended to function as a free-and-easy group,' Saul explained, as he knelt back to the floorboards. 'It was good.'

For a while she thought about his experiences,

the pleasure he had so obviously had, the interesting people he would have met.

'I must rethink my work:play ratio,' Gabrielle muttered. Her lounging against the door-jamb ceased, and she stood to attention. 'The moment we're out of here I shall reorganise my life,' she declared.

Saul shot her a discerning look. 'You're ready to ease up? You'll cut down on work? Actively delegate?'

'Um . . . yes,' she said, bemused by this sudden intensity.

He dusted off his hands and stood up. 'Then now's the time to talk about Anniversaries' future.'

Gabrielle stared at him. Her company's future? Her heart grew heavy. She had been so busy talking about the past, so busy listening to him talk, so busy liking him, she had never given a thought to the danger he represented. Two days ago the advancement of her company had been Number One in her mind, yet she had forgotten about it. How could that be?

'You do agree Anniversaries has a future?' she demanded, as fears of her shops being split up and sold off leapt out like ghouls from their graves and danced a monstrous dance before her.

'Yes, though not in the way you see it.'

'And what does that mean?' Gabrielle said sharply.

To be told her shops would continue was a relief,

yet a brief one. True, he had not struck the fatal blow, but he still remained capable of handing out a merciless thrashing, and she would be foolish to be too thankful, too soon.

'It's obvious you're stretched to the limit as far as personal supervision goes,' Saul stated, 'so——'

'You won't agree to my expansion?'

'I didn't say that. What I'm saying is——'

'That I'm to mark time. That Anniversaries has come to a full stop. That progress ends here. Thanks very much—for nothing!' She clenched her fists, her nails biting deep into her palms. 'I suspected that when you put the new properties on hold it was to be annihilation, and I was right,' Gabrielle said bitterly. 'Kevin believed you were thinking things over, but I knew——'

'Would you let me finish my sentence?' Saul rasped. 'Just one sentence?'

She glowered. 'Proceed.'

'Thanks. Like you, I believe Anniversaries should grow, and I'm with you on expansion all the way—except that I feel it should be in the form of franchises.'

'Franchises?' Gabrielle repeated dumbly.

'You provide the name, the know-how, the style, and the shop-owners put in a slug of cash and plenty of enthusiasm. You've agreed that other people have bright ideas, so, although the majority of the stock will be the same countrywide, why not allow the franchises to select some items for themselves? Then, if the goods take off, other branches can sell them as well. You'll still be running the show, but it'll be far more of a team effort,' Saul explained. 'And, while we're talking about teams, for heaven's sake train yourself some buyers. Shouldering the entire purchasing responsibility is not only crazy from the point of view of your personal workload, it also leaves the company alarmingly vulnerable. Suppose you're knocked down by a bus? Suppose you catch malaria? Suppose you——?'

'Get kidnapped?' Gabrielle put in.

'That as well,' he agreed drily.

She frowned. 'How would these franchises work?'

Saul had investigated the subject thoroughly, and his explanation was in detail and at length.

'Think about it, and about buyers,' he said, coming to the end.

'I will. Franchises don't sound such a bad idea,' she admitted, after a minute or two. 'In fact, they could be quite good.'   •

He squatted down to the floor again. 'But this isn't,' Saul said grimly. 'We have a problem here. The board's loose, but it sure as hell isn't going to lift out—not today. And maybe not tomorrow.' He looked up and sighed. 'We need to think again.' Abruptly he listened. 'Action stations. We're about to be invaded by those pains in the——'

'Necks?'

'I was thinking of three feet lower . . . Any news from Mr Vincent?' he enquired, when their captors walked in.

'Not yet. 'Course,' Jock sniggered, coming to loom over where they were sitting, like a malevolent beetle, 'if his business drags on you could be 'ere this time next week.'

Gabrielle's heart contracted, but when Saul sent her a 'take no notice' look of reassurance she smiled back.

'Suppose I increase my offer of cash?' Saul suggested.

The Scot readjusted his hold on the gun. 'Not interested.'

'To how much?' asked Phil, at the same time.

'Two thousand.'

'How would we get it?' the youth enquired, pound signs almost visibly revolving in his eyes.

'The pair of you would drive Gabby and me back to my hotel, where I'd collect my cheque-book.'

'Don't listen to 'im,' the older man snapped.

'Then you'd escort me to my bank, where——'

'Shut your mouth!'

'—I'd arrange to withdraw the cash. I'd hand over two thousand pounds in notes,' Saul continued, 'then——'

The Scot changed the revolver about and, in a swift, vicious downward swing, slammed the butt against Saul's temple.

'Shut it!'

Gabrielle gasped. The thud was sickening. His head snapped back by the force of the blow, Saul blinked and was forced to clutch at the arms of the chair in order to keep himself upright.

'Hell!' he breathed, his face contracted with pain.

'Another word, big boy, and you'll get a second one,' Jock threatened, relishing his power. He raised the gun. 'Or maybe you'd like another taste right now?'

Gabrielle leapt up. 'Leave him alone!'

The Scot laughed. 'And why should I?'

'Because I say so! You think you're tough, but there's nothing tough about hitting someone when they're masked or sitting down!' she cried, her eyes glittering with distaste. 'Take away the gun and what are you—just an ignorant, ill-mannered, cowardly *pygmy*!'

'Pygmy?' he repeated.

'The only reason you call Saul "big boy" is because you're stunted,' she declared. 'But call him big boy again and——'

Jock puffed out his chest. 'Big boy,' he taunted.

Anger had been building up inside her brick by taut brick, but now something inside Gabrielle snapped. Given the chance, she knew the bully would start his battering again—but not if she could stop him. Another blow would not be struck if she could keep Jock away.

'Get out of here!' she shouted, and hurled herself on him like a wild thing.

Taken by surprise, he shied defensively to one side. 'Watch it,' he protested.

'Be careful, Gabby,' Saul mumbled behind her, but the warning went unheeded.

Arms flailing like windmills, she batted and poked and prodded. She had never felt so enraged or so fiercely protective in her life.

'Out! Out!' she ordered.

For several seconds her victim stood firm, if bewildered, then abruptly he was doubling over and backing away. 'I'm going,' he yelped, but Gabrielle followed, relentlessly whamming and bamming and propelling him into the hallway, where he and Phil collided.

There was an untidy scramble for the door, a key turned, feet scuttled a hasty departure, and finally—silence. Tumbled-haired and panting, she hooked the wandering sweater back on to her shoulder.

'Thanks,' Saul said, and she turned to see him walking unsteadily towards her. 'You were wonderful,' he smiled, and opened wide his arms.

Rushing into them, Gabrielle laid her head against his shoulder and began to cry. A moment ago she could have fought armies, but reaction was setting in and her bravura had collapsed. Now she needed to be held close and comforted and caressed.

'It's OK,' Saul murmured, as the tears poured down her cheeks. He stroked her back. 'Gabby, it's OK.'

'No, no, it's not!' she sobbed. 'Jock hurt you, and he was going to hurt you again.'

'Only you made sure it didn't happen. And with a vengeance.' His lips were against her brow and she felt him smile. 'I thought you reckoned you were anti-violence?'

'I only pushed him,' she mumbled, and raised a tear-streaked face. 'How are you feeling?' she enquired anxiously.

'Not too bad. The blow sounded worse than it was. It stunned me for a while, but——' Saul felt his temple '—apart from leaving me with what could be a beauty of a bump—that's about all.'

Gabrielle eyed him doubtfully. Even if no great damage had been done, he still looked pale and drawn.

'I think you should sit down,' she told him.

'I think you could be right,' he said in ready agreement, and sank on to the chaise-longue, drawing her down beside him.

'When Jock was making his getaway I ought to have tried to snatch the gun,' she sighed, as she recovered.

'And I should have helped you,' Saul said ruefully.

'There was a chance, but we didn't take it. Yet if we had and there had been a struggle, perhaps the gun would've gone off and——' her voice dropped to a cathedral hush '—we wouldn't have been sitting here now!'

'But we are, sugar.' He stroked his knuckles down her cheek. 'We are,' he repeated.

Saul kissed the corner of her mouth, and her nose, and her brow, then, with an incoherent murmur, he returned to her mouth. The previous kisses had been gestures of comfort, but now his lips opened on hers and he began kissing her hungrily and deeply. Gabrielle wound her arms around his neck. It felt wonderful to be close to him, to stretch her body against his, to taste him. So wonderful. So right. Everything had changed . . . yet nothing had changed. The chemistry which had first brought them together remained as potent as ever. But the attraction was not just a chemical combustion, there was more. Much more. Suddenly Gabrielle knew why she had been so ferociously defensive, she understood what had made her fight off his attacker. I love him, she thought dazedly. Still.

Saul bent his head to kiss the alluring inches of skin between her earlobe and the low neckline of her sweater. The angora had slipped again and his lips were warm on her shoulder. Desire caught her in its dizzy spell. Via her bloodstream, it sensitised her lips, tightened her nipples, created an emptiness which needed to be filled. Gabrielle wanted them to be naked. She wanted the sweet torture of his fingers on her skin. She wanted——

Saul drew back. 'No,' he said. Breathing hard, he stared at her. 'Hell, I must be concussed,' he remarked, with an attempt at humour which, for once, failed to hit the mark. 'This is neither the time nor the place——'

'You're right,' she agreed, and promptly moved away.

If he was out of his mind, so was she! To love him was one thing, but to do something about it was a vastly different proposition. For a start, she had no good reason to suppose the feeling was reciprocated. Yes, he had been kissing her, but gratitude and routine lust could account for that . . . Gabrielle shot him a covert glance. The pivot upon which any relationship between them must revolve was whether she could forgive and forget what he had done eight years ago—and she did not think she could. His past behaviour would always be there between them, a poisoned wedge.

'Why don't you lie down for a while?' she suggested. 'I can work on the floorboard and keep an ear out for visitors at the same time.'

'You're sure?'

Gabrielle nodded. 'I'm sure.'

To her surprise, Saul slept for several hours. Worried now that the blow could have had some unknown harmful effect, she made constant checks, but each time he was sleeping peacefully. And when he awoke mid-evening his colour had returned.

'You look much better.' Gabrielle smiled as he wolfed down sandwiches and coffee.

'I feel it. Any progress with the floorboard?'

'None.'

Saul munched reflectively. 'I'm going to have a try at getting the gun away from Jock,' he muttered.

'No!'

'Gabby, it shouldn't be too difficult, not if we choreograph everything. The bastard's going to be mighty wary of you from now on, so if you started another argument, I could catch him off guard. Phil didn't come to the rescue before, he just hopped around in the background, so obviously he's not a fighter.'

'But he is interested in the money,' she said, in a rush. 'And Jock wouldn't be so hostile when you talk about it unless he was tempted, too. Give them a bit longer,' she pleaded. 'I'm sure they'll accept your offer.'

'But do we have a bit longer to give?' Saul demanded. 'This Vincent character doesn't appear to be in a rush, but there's no guarantee he won't turn up any time. Besides, even if the prospect of ready cash does make their hot little hands sweat, Jock and Phil can't be so dim they won't consider the downside—the risks they would be taking in publicly carting us from the hotel to the bank.'

Gabrielle frowned. What he said made sense. Yet the dangers involved in him attempting to disarm the Scot filled her with dread.

'Phil's almost convinced we're not the Arnotts,' she said, 'and when you called me Gabby this afternoon I'm certain Jock noticed. He's going to think about it and realise that, as you were dazed at the time, it must be my real name.'

'Is he? I wouldn't bet on it.' Saul pushed his plate aside. 'Let's discuss this tomorrow.'

For the remainder of the evening, he was quiet. Their discussion might have been postponed, but in the interim he appeared to be doing some serious thinking. Even when Gabrielle said she was tired and ready for bed, he continued to brood.

'You go,' he said, bidding her goodnight. 'I'll join you later.'

As she lay in the darkness, cameos from the day painted themselves in her mind. Once again, she saw Saul dropping a one-liner which had made her laugh. Saul earnestly explaining the benefits of the franchise scheme. Saul's head being whipped back by the cruel metal uppercut. Saul opening wide his arms . . . Gabrielle peered at the luminous fingers on her watch. It was well past midnight, and yet he remained in the living-room. For how long? she wondered, yawning. He could not stay up all night.

Gabrielle awoke with a start. The pencil of yellow light had gone from beneath the door and it was pitch black—yet instinct told her she was alone. Switching on the lamp, she again checked the time. Three o'clock. Where was Saul? She crawled out of bed, pulled the sweater over her head, and padded to the door. In the living-room a pale haze of moonlight silvered the armchair where he sat with long legs stretched out, but shadows made it impossible to tell whether or not he was sleeping. Treading quietly, she approached.

'Go back to bed,' he said all of a sudden, startling her.

Gabrielle walked closer. 'You come to bed,' she entreated. 'You can't be comfortable.'

'I am.'

'Which is why it's the middle of the night and you're wide awake? OK, so you slept earlier, but you must be tired by now.'

He sat up. 'I'm staying here.'

'Saul, for the past two nights you've slept in the bed and slept well,' she coaxed.

A muscle clenched in his jaw. 'Exhaustion knocked me out the first night, but yesterday I spent most of my time pacing the floor out here.'

Gabrielle's eyes widened. 'You did? But I

thought——'

'What did you think?' he demanded roughly. 'That I can lie beside you and not bloody react? Well, I can't! Have you any idea how close I was to making love to you earlier, and how much self-restraint it needed to tear myself away?' He glared at her through the dim light. 'And knowing you wanted me as much as I wanted you didn't make it any easier.'

'I—I wanted you?' she faltered.

Saul's eyes locked with hers. 'Gabby, you can pretend all you like,' he said, in a low harsh voice, 'but the truth is, there's a helluva lot of unfinished business between us.'

CHAPTER EIGHT

THE air seemed to throb.

'What kind of unfinished business?' Gabrielle enquired carefully.

'Every kind! Emotional, physical—you name it. After eight damn years you and I still *affect* each other. That's the price we've had to pay for our passion.' Anger was radiating from him. 'Maybe we should make love. Maybe that'll exorcise the demons. Maybe then I'll be able to get on with living the rest of my life.'

She gazed at him through the shadows. He sounded so anguished, so overwrought, she knew—even though he might resent it deeply—that he loved her, too. Hope soared. Hope fell. What difference did his love make? None. Or did it? Maybe she *could* forget. Maybe she *could* put the past behind her.

'Relax,' Saul said curtly, when she frowned. 'I'm only offering a theory. I'm not about to have my wicked way with you.'

'Why not?' Gabrielle's chin rose. 'Are you afraid you'll make me pregnant?'

Her response clearly surprised him, and for a moment he was silent.

'That's one of the reasons,' he grated. 'But if I did, I can't see a child superseding Anniversaries in your affections, can you?'

Gabrielle's mouth thinned. That was unfair. She had told him she was going to ease up. She had vowed she would reorganise her life. She had admitted her priorities were all wrong.

'And what about you?' she slammed back, aggressively playing tit-for-tat. 'Would you be happy to be a daddy?'

A strange look came into his face. 'As a matter of fact, I'd be delighted.'

'Huh, the pundits are right, time does alter everything,' she said nastily. 'What a pity you didn't feel this way eight years ago!'

'You have no idea what my feelings were then,' he asserted quietly.

Gabrielle set scornful hands on her hips. 'On the contrary, you made your attitude abundantly clear. When I asked what you'd do if you knew I was having a baby——'

'I said I'd say "goodbye",' Saul rasped, displaying a total recall of one of the most traumatic moments in her life. 'I said it once, just once, and it was a joke.'

'Some joke!'

'Have you never come out with anything stupid?' he demanded. 'Something you wish like hell you'd never said and could cancel? Eight years ago I was young and insecure. You have to allow me some latitude.'

'You didn't seem so damned insecure to me!' Gabrielle retorted.

'Of course not. I don't suppose I appeared particularly young, either. But you were only nineteen, what experience did you have of people and the way they behave? What did you know about looking beyond the façade, recognising bravado?' He left his chair and walked to the window. 'I was approaching thirty, but I'd yet to start a proper job. And once I'd started, I wasn't sure if I'd be able to hold it down. Up until then I'd had a disastrous employment record,' he said, gazing out into the darkness. 'On all sides my contemporaries were outstripping me; not only in terms of their careers, but in their personal lives. Several of my friends were married and already had kids. And what had I achieved until I met you? A few tawdry affairs.' Saul turned to face her. 'At times I felt horribly lightweight, woefully inadequate.'

She flung him a sceptical look. 'But you had the opportunity to have a child, and what did you do?' she demanded. 'You made damn sure it'd never happen!'

He shook his head. 'I didn't make any decision. There was no time. One week you told me you were pregnant. Ten days later you miscarried.'

'And that was mere chance?' she enquired bitterly.

Saul sighed. 'What else?'

Gabrielle's look changed from scepticism to angry disbelief. 'Psychologists say we are continually reconstructing the past, but you take it to the limit!'

'What are you talking about?'

'I'm talking about an evening when you dined with your uncle and his friends, and we spoke on the telephone. I'm talking about you suggesting, very casually and cleverly, that I might like to consume alcohol. I'm talking about you insisting I take a hot bath. I'm talking about——'

Gabrielle stopped dead. What *was* she talking about? Her accusations hung in the air, totally ludicrous. For all these years she had heaped the blame on him, but in a sudden insight she saw that, where reality had gone straight on, at some point in the road she had taken a sharp left. Saul had not promoted gin, nor, as far as she could remember, specified any particular drink. He had, with half his mind on the activity taking place around him, made a random suggestion. And as for her taking a bath—he had never given commands there, either.

Gabrielle went cold. Even as a besotted nineteen-year-old, she had not been so blindly subservient as to do everything he might propose with never a thought. Even at nineteen, she had not been utterly naïve. The cold curled icy fingers around her heart. She must have been aware of the dangers of her actions that evening. She had to have had an inkling of possible consequences!

'Doesn't it seem strange to you that I was all bad and you were all good?' Saul rasped, in an uncanny parallel of the thoughts which swirled in her head. 'Sorry, life isn't like that.'

'No,' she muttered, but he was not listening.

'So, I was responsible for the miscarriage? I engineered it because I didn't want your pregnancy to proceed? I killed your baby?' he said, the memory of her accusation adding a hard, ragged edge to his voice. 'Then why the hell did I go to the hospital and beg to be told the sex of my child? *My* child,' he insisted. '*My* son.'

Hot tears brimmed in her eyes. 'The baby was a boy?' Gabrielle whispered, sinking down on to the chaise-longue.

A terrible sadness swept over her. At the time the nurses had refused to give her the information she had so desperately asked for. They had pretended not to know. Lack of details was supposed to help her forget more quickly.

'But if you wanted a child, why were you so—so cheerful after I'd lost it?' she enquired, in bewilderment.

'I didn't actively *want* one, not then and there. I didn't get you pregnant on purpose,' Saul said harshly. 'Yet once the baby was an entity, I discovered I cared about it. Cared strongly—then and later.'

'Later?'

'Do you think you're the only one who, over the years, has looked at kids of two, three, five, six, whatever, and wondered what our child would have been like?'

A lump lodged in her throat. 'You've done that, too?' Gabrielle asked chokily.

'Often. I've carried him on my shoulders. I've taught him to kick a ball. I see him with your red hair and my blue eyes. A spunky kid.' Saul rubbed his knuckles together. 'As for being cheerful, it would have been foolish to deny that life had become a lot simpler again, and—and damage limitation seemed important. The admission that my world had been torn apart, too, would have got us nowhere.'

'Being cheerful was a pretence?'

'It was my way of dealing with a rotten situation. I laughed, you sobbed,' he muttered. 'We were both miserable.'

'But——'

'It's not only clowns who play the fool to hide their pain,' he thrust, with sudden savagery.

In the silence which followed, Gabrielle curled and uncurled her toes in the shaggy carpet. He had given her a lot to think about. For instance, when he had said that at nineteen she had not known about people he had been right—but she had been aware of a few fundamentals.

'I've always told myself it was you who didn't want the baby.' She swallowed hard and faced the stark reality. 'But it wasn't, it was *me*. The tears I shed afterwards weren't from despair, they were from guilt!'

'You felt guilty because you were relieved about the miscarriage? But relief was natural,' Saul protested. 'It's one helluva shock for a girl in her teens to find herself pregnant. You'd just started at university and——'

'You don't understand.' She pushed her toes deeper into the pile. 'I felt guilty because when I drank the gin that evening and had the bath, I did so hoping they would solve the problem. You were at the end of a phone a hundred and fifty miles away, and in no position to gauge the seriousness of what was happening. But I could. I knew something had gone wrong, and I deliberately encouraged it to get worse. I didn't admit it to myself, either then or afterwards, but——' her voice cracked, '—*I* got rid of that baby.'

'No. You would have miscarried in any case.' Saul came to sit beside her. 'I spoke to the doctor, and he explained how it had been inevitable. Something about the egg not being properly lodged in the womb.'

'He told me that, too, but——'

He placed his hand over hers. 'There are no buts, Gabby,' he said, sounding very calm, very certain. 'Perhaps gin and hot baths can have some effect in certain circumstances, I don't know, but I've always understood their efficiency to be an old wives' tale.'

For a long moment she looked at him, then she nodded. She believed the doctor. And she believed him.

'I mentioned reconstructing the past. I seem to have done it in other areas as well,' Gabrielle confessed. 'I was convinced you never lifted a finger when we lived together, and I did everything—but it wasn't like that.'

'You did a heck of a lot!' Saul protested.

'Only because I insisted on it. But you built those shelves, and you regularly made us coffee, and——'

'I put out the trash?' he grinned.

Gabrielle nodded. 'You were very useful. Then and afterwards.'

'Afterwards?'

'Do you know what kept me going through the difficult times with Anniversaries? You. Whenever I hit a hurdle, I used to grit my teeth and think "I'll show him".'

Saul raised a droll brow. 'Glad to be of service.'

'My hatred of you was strong and solid,' she said, with a shamefaced smile, 'something to hang on to.'

'You said *was*. Does that mean that somewhere along the way you relented?'

'Time does take the sting out of things.'

'But you never forgot about me?'

'No.'

'And what's been the stimulus recently?'

'I'm not sure there has been one. I think I continue partly through momentum, and——' Gabrielle looked down at the strong brown fingers intertwined with hers '—partly because Anniversaries is all I have in my life. I've shut out most everything else.'

Saul's eyes narrowed. 'You're not telling me you really have lived like a nun all these years?'

'No. There have been men—one or two—but they were there on my terms. As soon as they showed the first sign of closing in on the relationship, I got out.'

'Ah, yes,' he drawled, and she heard the hurt in his voice. 'I remember it well.'

Gabrielle felt a pang of regret. 'The other day,' she said slowly, 'I told you I'd made a major mistake. You thought I meant moving in with you, but I didn't. I was referring to moving out. Yes, things were sticky between us, but I never planned to leave. It just happened.'

Saul shook his head. 'Nothing just happens.'

She hesitated. 'True' she admitted. 'I was getting out before you threw me out.'

'And why would I throw out a girl who combined a beautiful face and body with an enquiring mind and fantastic sex?' he demanded. 'When I fell in love with you—no,' he stopped himself. 'I didn't fall in love. Love knocked me down, ran me over, got me by the throat and shook me until I rattled. Why else do you think I was in such a state that I went ahead and made love to you without taking the usual precautions?' he asked, when she frowned. 'Sexual choices are rarely rational or expedient, but I did know the facts of life!' Saul gave a bleak laugh. 'I also knew that if I didn't have you, I'd die. So, in the heat of the moment——'

Her heart performed a somersault. 'It was that bad?'

'It was,' he confirmed.

'I wish I'd realised how strongly you felt.'

'I told you!'

'You didn't,' Gabrielle rejected. 'There was a lot of verbal horseplay about me being the love of your life, but you never spoke about it in any serious way.'

He sighed. 'You're right. I guess owning up to strong feelings scared me, and being flippant was a kind of . . . emotional camouflage.'

'A complete one! If I ever attempted to argue, you'd always make me laugh—or start making love.' She gave a disgusted growl. 'It was *infuriating*.'

Saul laughed, then he sobered. 'I wasn't too happy about having rows at that stage. Insecurity again. I thought a quarrel meant it was going to be the end of everything——' he ran a slow finger over the back of her hand '—and even though I avoided out-and-out fighting, for you and me, it was.' He gave her a frowning glance. 'Whatever made you think I intended to throw you out?'

'Well . . .' Gabrielle began to explain how she had wondered if she was just one in a line of girls, about how their worlds had seemed so different, about her being convinced she lacked the necessary sophistication. 'In retrospect, it's clear I was far too impressed by you,' she said. 'You were nine years older, and very good-looking, and——'

'Are you impressed now?'

'No-o.'

'I'm still nine years older.'

'Ye-s.'

Saul slapped a theatrical hand to his brow. 'Don't tell me. The prince has mutated into an ugly old toad?'

'Stop fishing for compliments,' Gabrielle grinned, and poked him in the ribs. 'I'm impressed by your achievements, but I'm no longer dazzled by you as a person.'

'Pity.'

'No, it's not. It's healthy!'

Saul made a face. 'I guess so.'

'If you felt so strongly about me, about us, why did you make no attempt to get in touch when I left?' she queried.

He gave a long-drawn-out sigh. 'Basically because I didn't know what the hell I was going to say, or how I could mend the situation. I lifted the phone to ring your parents and ask to speak to you several times. I even caught the train and ended up outside their house on one occasion, but I spoke to one of the neighbours who told me you'd gone away, and after that I—I chickened out. I felt lousy about what had happened and, heaven knows, I didn't want us to end, but I couldn't seem to come up with the right solution.' He subjected her to a long, level look. 'I did wonder about proposing.'

'I'm glad you didn't,' she said quickly. 'I was much too young to be married.'

'So—no ill-feelings?' Saul asked.

'None.'

He gave a broad grin. 'Thanks.'

Thank *you*, Gabrielle thought. Thank you for making me look at the past clearly. Thank you for showing me the error of my ways. And thank you for loving me.

She gave him a teasing sideways glance. 'You said there were several reasons why you won't be having your wicked way with me. Please could you tell me the others?'

'Why?' he demanded, abruptly wary.

Gabrielle spread her fingers on his thigh. 'I'd just like to know.'

'Don't flirt!'

'Why not?' she asked, grinning.

'You know why. Further reasons for me keeping my distance,' Saul said, firmly removing her hand. 'With Jock and Phil liable to come in at any moment this is, as I've said before, the wrong time and the wrong place for any . . . intimacy.'

'They've never disturbed us in the middle of the night before,' she pointed out, but he ignored her.

'Plus, there's every chance making love would not exorcise one damn thing.'

Gabrielle smiled. She agreed with him. Wholeheartedly. If they conspired in that incandescence, that loss of control, that endless pleasure, then—whatever his misgivings about her obsession with Anniversaries—he would be forced to admit he loved her.

'And where would that leave us?' she enquired, a picture of innocence.

'It would——' Saul repelled the thought. 'We've talked long enough. It's high time you went back to bed.'

'I will, when you've kissed me goodnight.' Gabrielle leaned against him. 'Just one kiss?'

'I'd rather not.'

Before he could stop her, she knelt up on the chaise-longue and straddled him.

'For someone who used to be so flippant, you've become horribly stodgy. One little kiss isn't going to hurt,' she murmured.

'On the contrary, it could do a great deal of damage,' he retaliated, as she slid her fingers between the buttons on his shirt. He held himself rigid. 'Would you kindly go?'

Gabrielle rubbed at the curls of dark hair on his chest, delighting in the roughness beneath her fingers. 'I understood there was nothing you liked better than a full-breasted young woman leaning——'

He gripped her hips to move her away, but when the angora rode up and he found himself clasping smooth, silky flesh Saul reared back as if he had been burned.

'You're naked underneath that sweater!' he protested.

She opened wide her eyes. 'I didn't want to be accused of being prissy again.'

'You're not. No way. Just go to bed,' he implored.

'Just kiss me.'

'I don't want to.'

'Sorry, Mr O'Connor,' Gabrielle grinned, 'your body language contradicts that statement.'

'So I'm aroused.' He swallowed down a laboured breath. 'What the hell do you expect?'

'A kiss?'

Saul lunged forward and placed a peck at the end of her nose. 'There.'

'It won't do.' She slid her hand across his chest and touched his nipple with the tip of her finger. 'I want a proper one.'

As he looked at her, his defences crumbled. 'And I want you,' he said huskily. 'Sugar, I want you so much.'

The teasing, the tantalising had gone. 'Kiss me, Saul,' she begged. 'Please.'

He slid his hands beneath the angora sweater and curled them around her waist, drawing her closer and settling her astride him. Then he spread his hands on her back and, holding her in position, he began to kiss her. They were fevered, burning kisses. Kisses which seemed to sear her very soul. Gabrielle raised an arm and curled her fingers tightly in the thick dark hair on the top of his head.

'You used to do that before,' Saul murmured, not taking his mouth from hers.

His hands moved beneath the sweater to caress the round sides of her breasts, then he trailed his fingers forward, forward, forward, until—in a moment of ecstasy—he touched the pointy tips. She gasped, and the heady, wonderful, floating feelings began to build. Saul caressed her, stroking and rubbing, until, with a murmur of protest, he pushed aside the fluffy wool and began to suck and lick at her nipples.

'And you used to do that before,' she sighed, feeling like a diver rocketing up for air.

'Oh, sugar,' he groaned, 'I'd give anything to be able to take you to bed right now.'

'You can,' she murmured. 'We aren't going to have any visitors, and as for birth control—I learned my lesson and now I——'

Her words were stopped mid-sentence by Saul placing his hand over her mouth. No visitors, she had just insisted, but noises at the door belied her claim. The key was being turned. Frozen in horror, Gabrielle stared at him—then hastily covered herself up. What did this departure from the routine mean? she wondered in alarm. Did

Jock intend to take revenge for her humiliation of him, by pouncing while they were asleep? Could the dire Mr Vincent have arrived from abroad? As Saul lowered his hand, she slid silently from his knee. He pointed, indicating for her to stay where she was, then made his way noiselessly across the room. In the hallway, he halted. The key had ceased to rattle, and all was still. Shoulders tense, energy coiled, he waited for someone to enter.

One minute passed and then two, but the door did not open. No intruder appeared. Frowning, Saul took quiet steps forward and stealthily turned the knob. A moment later he swivelled, beckoning for Gabrielle to join him.

'Get dressed,' he said, into her ear. 'I don't know why, or what's happening, but someone's unlocked the door and gone away again.'

Swiftly, she obeyed his instructions.

'What now?' she hissed, returning to his side.

'You stay here while I take a look outside. If everything seems OK, I'll go down to the bottom of the stairs. I'll whistle once if the coast is clear, and then you follow me. But if you should hear any other noise, close the door immediately and keep your head well down,' he warned. 'This could be some kind of a trick.'

Cautiously, Saul opened the door, then looked back at her and winked. Gabrielle's reply was a tremulous grin. Her heart thudding, she watched him step out on to the landing. Please let everything be all right, she prayed, as he disappeared into the darkness. Please don't let anything happen to him. Please keep him safe. I love him and, even if he's doubtful about it, he loves me, and after eight long years apart we *need* each other.

For what seemed like interminable minutes Gabrielle waited; then, as she was beginning to panic and fear the worst, she heard a low whistle. Briskly, she stepped out over the threshold, and gasped as cold night air hit her full in the face. Cocooned indoors, she had forgotten about the winter, the weather—forgotten about everything except herself and Saul. But now, in the light of a full moon, she saw frost glistening on the roofs and a treacherous layer of ice on the wooden steps. If she had realised the outside temperature was below zero, she would have worn her sweatshirt and ribbed tights, and a few more layers as well, she thought, as she carefully made her way down to where Saul stood.

'I haven't seen anyone,' he whispered, taking hold of her hand.

Quickly he led her across the gap between the stable buildings and the house and, keeping in its lee, took her forward. Reaching the corner, he stopped, peered round and nodded. All was dark and silent. The way ahead looked clear. As they crossed the square of gravel in front of the house,

Gabrielle gazed about her. On three sides parkland stretched out in the moonlight, while straight ahead she saw a tree-lined drive which wound off into the distance. Apprehensively her eyes searched the shadows, but nothing moved.

'OK?' Saul whispered.

She gave a giddy smile. 'I'm fine.'

'We're not out of this yet,' he cautioned, and pointed to the drive. 'We run, at the side, under the trees and keeping in the shadows. We run like hell. We run until we hit a road. You go first and I'll be right behind you. Ready, steady, go!'

At the command Gabrielle streaked off, her elbows moving like pistons, the satin boots crunching on the frozen grass. Following the curve of the drive, she passed a pond lacquered a ghostly silver, ran beside sombre heaps of frost-rimed timber. Once or twice her foot skidded, but she recovered and kept on running, comforted by the sound of Saul pounding along behind her. With him close she would traverse the world, if need be. Despite the bitter cold, soon she was sweating. On and on she ran, her breath making white clouds in the frosty air. A stitch was beginning to form in her side when, blessedly, she saw the road. No more than a narrow hedge-lined country lane, it represented civilisation and—she grinned— freedom.

'Safe?' she demanded breathlessly, as they hit the tarmac.

Saul gathered her up into a hug.

'Safe,' he panted.

'Thank goodness, thank goodness.' Without warning, headlamps swung around a bend, abruptly changing secure dark into arc-lit jeopardy. 'Oh, no!' she squeaked.

As the car braked, stopping within yards of them, Gabrielle blinked like a rabbit against the glare. Safe? Her stomach hollowed. They had spoken too soon. They had taken too much for granted. Was this Jock and Phil, bent on recapture? Had this taste of freedom been nothing more than the appalling Mr Vincent playing a diabolical game?

Saul steered her behind him, then raised a hand to his eyes. 'It's the police,' he said.

Weak and shaky with relief, she went with him to speak to the uniformed sergeant and constable.

'Jump in,' the sergeant instructed, when first explanations had been made. He listened to more of what Saul had to say, digested the details, then set about contacting his headquarters. 'The house must be searched, but if that Jock character's toting a gun, then our boys'll need to be armed, too,' he said. 'I dare say him and his mate'll be miles away by now, but there's no point in taking chances.'

'We told them they'd picked up the wrong people,' Gabrielle said, when the message had been sent. 'Phil was always inclined to believe us, but

Jock refused to listen.' She grinned. 'But obviously it penetrated his thick head at last.'

'You reckon they released you because they realised they'd made a mistake?' the constable enquired.

She frowned. 'Didn't they?'

'Far be it from me to decry your powers of persuasion,' the young man replied, with an appreciative smile at her shape revealed by the low-cut sweater and short skirt, 'but I doubt they were responsible.'

'Then what was?' asked Saul.

Now the sergeant took over, resting an arm on the back of his seat. 'Carl Vincent, the bloke who owns the house, is a recognised villain—but a canny one. We've known for a long while that he's been mixed up with drugs, though knowing it and proving it are two different things,' he said ruefully. 'As you guessed, he spends a lot of his time in Spain and, like us, the authorities over there have endless files detailing his endless offences.'

'What kind of offences?' Saul interrupted.

'Drug-peddling, smuggling, plus intimidation and assault—Vincent's a nasty piece of work.'

Gabrielle clung on to Saul's hand. 'Then we were fortunate not to have met him?'

'Very. Anyhow, yesterday someone talked and the Spanish police finally nailed him. He was arrested and put into jail.' The sergeant chuckled. 'I understand with the evidence there is piled up against him, that's one gentleman who won't be walking the streets again this century.'

Saul frowned. 'So you figure Jock and Phil were alerted and they decided that, with the boss out of action, they'd better let us go?'

'I do.'

'Has to be that way, sir,' said the constable. He grinned at Gabrielle. 'Sorry.'

'Do you think you're likely to catch them?' she asked, as they set off for the police station. 'Jock was grisly, but I quite liked Phil.'

'If they have a criminal record, chances are we'll pick them up. But if you put in your statement that the boy did you no harm, it'll count in his favour.' The constable looked back over his shoulder. 'Not one of these girls who fall in love with their kidnappers, are you?' he asked.

She shared a grin with Saul. 'No.'

'I've never heard of these Arnotts,' the sergeant mused, 'but if they've nipped off with part of a haul, the London boys might know them. Still, we'll organise that later.'

'Organising' took time, and it was nine o'clock in the morning when Gabrielle and Saul returned to the mews. In the interim many questions had been asked, statements taken, Carl Vincent's property had been searched—but, as prophesied, their captors had vanished. Later the sergeant's wife had made them breakfast. And later still a car was provided to ferry them home.

'Are you stopping off here, too?' Gabrielle

asked Saul, as the taxi halted on the cobbles.

'No,' he said gently. 'You're exhausted and so am I. I'll carry on to the hotel, that way we'll both get some much needed rest.' He smiled at the regret she had been unable to mask. 'But I'll be back at seven to take you out for the biggest and best celebration dinner.' He kissed her on the lips. 'See you later, sugar.'

'See you later,' she sighed.

CHAPTER NINE

GABRIELLE had just stepped out of the shower when the doorbell buzzed. Hastily drying herself, she wrapped a towel around her and wet-footprinted her way along the hall.

'Who is it?' she called.

The alarm was on and the door secured with bolts and chain, but she was taking no chances. And, if this was someone selling encyclopedia or religion, she would send them promptly on their way.

'Me.' There was a pause. 'Saul.'

Holding on to the precariously knotted towel, she fumbled to let him in. 'But it's only six o—heavens!'

As she had turned the lock, bells had begun pealing out everywhere—shrilling, blaring, claxoning—at full volume. The ear-splitting din bounced off the walls, shivered the windows, almost raised the roof. Gabrielle blinked. Now she knew what it must feel like to stand alongside Big Ben.

'Where are the switches?' Saul shouted.

Dazedly she looked at him, then swung a hand. 'Er—in the cloaks cupboard. Just here.'

179

He ditched the armful of gifts he was carrying and plunged in, frantically elbowing coats and mackintoshes aside. 'Which section governs the door?' he demanded.

Gabrielle gazed at the control box with its red lights and multitude of levers. Think, girl, *think*. The service engineer was very exact. He repeated the procedure several times.

'Er—the top one,' she said.

He pressed a button, but the bells continued to jangle.

'Try again,' Saul yelled.

'The second one down?'

It was the fourth, and by the time the racket had finally been doused she was sure that not only had her neighbours and everyone in Kensington been alerted, but most of the dead in London must have been raised as well.

'You did tell me seven,' Gabrielle said, into the ensuing silence—which somehow sounded as loud as the bells.

'I couldn't keep away.' Saul stepped out from the hurly-burly of the cloaks cupboard and ran a smoothing hand over his hair. 'Tell me, if I'd waited until then, would I still have made your chimes ring?' he enquired, in a low husky voice.

Gabrielle hitched up the droopy towel. 'Definitely.'

He crooked an arm around her waist and bent to press his mouth to her bare shoulder, licking away a rogue droplet of water. 'Then we'd better take the necessary action.' He smiled deep into her eyes. 'Yes?'

'Yes,' she said, deliciously aware of conducting a two-level conversation.

His arm tightened. 'Now?' he murmured.

'No.' It took an effort, but she removed herself from his orbit. 'First, I have something to tell you.'

Saul heaved a mammoth sigh, then obediently followed her into the living-room. He had waited eight years to make love to her again. He supposed he could, if necessary, wait a few minutes longer.

'Tell away,' he said, when they were sitting together on the sofa.

'I've been in touch with my office——'

'So soon?' he complained.

'Yes, and I've done three things. Number one, I've arranged for advertisements to be placed in the weekend papers for buyers for Anniversaries. Number two, I've spoken to Kevin about the franchises——'

'Does he agree?'

'He thinks it's a great idea. And I've advised him that we'll be meeting with you in the near future to thrash out the details,' she continued. 'Number three, I've instructed my secretary to leave my diary free for the entire month of May, because I shall be going on holiday.' Gabrielle grinned. 'I rather fancy the Caribbean.'

'So, once again, you'll be running barefoot

along a shore?' Saul grinned. He lifted his hand and slowly traced the shape of her lips with his finger. 'How about staying in bed at the weekends, sugar—with me? Or going to bed——' he unpeeled the towel and drew long, tanned fingers down her shoulders, over her breasts, beyond her waist, across her stomach, to clasp her thighs '—at six ten in the evening, again with me?'

'It sounds wonderful,' Gabrielle murmured, opening eyes which had been closed with the rapture of his touch.

Saul picked her up in his arms and carried her through to the bedroom, where he laid her gently on the bed. A moment later he was stretched out naked between the sheets like a splendid golden-skinned animal, pulling her down on top of him and kissing her again and again.

'Gabby,' he said, as his eager mouth sought her breasts, 'Gabby, I do love you.'

She stroked the marble-smooth muscles of his shoulders, trailed her fingers through the dark hair on his chest.

'And I love you. I always have and I always will.'

He rolled her off him to catch at her nipples, rubbing with the pad of his thumbs around and around in a searching, rhythmic pressure, until she cried out aloud. Gabrielle arched closer. She felt her body burgeoning, opening to his touch, and as he slithered a hand between her thighs and dipped a long finger into the satiny moistness he had inspired, she cried out again.

'Sugar,' he murmured, and moved to cover her body with his.

He slid into her, so swiftly, so deeply, he seemed to touch the innermost core of her being. Gabrielle felt herself swirling, reaching, rising and dissolving. She began to move her hips with his and a rhythm was established, a rhythm which wrenched deep groans of ecstasy from her—and from him.

'Sugar,' he muttered, as the rhythm compulsively increased. 'Sugar, sugar, sugar . . .'

Among the gifts Saul had brought—and forgotten—was a bottle of champagne, though it was mid-evening before they found time to drink it.

'To us,' he grinned, raising his glass. 'And to our visit to the Caribbean.'

Gabrielle pulled the sheet more decorously over her breasts. '*Our* visit?' she queried.

'Betancourts might not be too pleased at me taking leave so soon, but every man's entitled to his honeymoon. Hell,' he complained, 'I'm doing this the wrong way round. You will marry me, won't you? Gabby, you *must*!' Saul insisted, suddenly perturbed.

Serenely, she sipped the champagne. 'Is this an order from my new boss?'

'A command. And he won't take no for an answer.'

'Then what can I say but—yes?'

Glasses were discarded in favour of kisses—and the champagne had lost some of its bubbles by the time they returned to it later.

'Did you book a table for dinner?' Gabrielle asked, tardily remembering what had been planned.

He shook his head. 'I was going to ask if you had a favourite place, but——' Saul grinned '—I figure no restaurant could compete with the celebration we're having here.'

'None,' she agreed, as he filled her glass again. 'Does that hurt?' she asked, stretching out her fingers to touch the bump on his temple. As he had foretold, it was a de-luxe edition.

'Only when I'm standing up. And how about you? How are you feeling?' He raked her with anxious eyes. 'Does having your burglar alarm switched on denote an attack of the reactionary jitters?'

Gabrielle gave a rueful smile. 'I have a few,' she confessed. 'I know no one's likely to break in again, but somehow the house doesn't feel as safe as it did before. What I need is my own personal bodyguard living in.' She tilted her head. 'I don't suppose you know of anyone who'd be interested?'

'Funny you should ask. There's a guy who's checking out of his hotel this evening. Think he'll do?'

'Perfectly.'

'How about putting this house on the market, and we buy a new place together?' Saul suggested, as they drank champagne.

'Good idea.' She nestled closer. 'A month ago I could have murdered the entire board, but now I'm so glad Betancourts scoured the world and hauled *you* in to be their chief executive.'

The corner of his mouth tweaked. 'It wasn't exactly like that.'

'No?' Gabrielle asked curiously.

He shook his head. 'OK, when you left me I didn't follow, but the moment your name appeared in the newspapers I sat up and took notice. Every morning I searched for snippets—I even ordered every single English paper when I was in the States, scared I might miss something—until eventually I saw reports about your tie-in with Betancourts. At that point it seemed like a good idea to learn more about the conglomerate.'

'Because of me?' she said, in astonishment.

'Yes. Oh, I told myself my interest was casual—that you were just a girl I'd once known and it would be intriguing to find something out about your connections—but subconsciously there was a lot more to it.' Saul put his glass aside. 'I said that at twenty-eight I was aware of my contemporaries' being married, and as I moved up my thirties the awareness grew. It wasn't that I clung to being a bachelor, it was simply a case of never meeting anyone I felt I could share the rest of my life with. I came close once, but at the last

moment I shied away.' His blue eyes met hers.
'You were the only woman I'd ever really loved,
and at the back of my mind was the feeling that I
needed to see you again. Not because I still cared.
Just to try and discover what it was that had
attracted me so much.'

'But you didn't need to join Betancourts in order
to see me!' Gabrielle protested.

'I didn't intend to.' He frowned. 'At least,
I don't think I did. What happened was that
when I'd studied the conglomerate I could see
glaring faults in the way it functioned, plus—even
with a cursory look—solutions to some of the
difficulties. I wrote to the board with a few
suggestions and, what d'you know, they begged me
to join them.'

'It was the smartest thing they ever
did!'

'And the smartest thing *I* ever did was
fixing a meeting with you! The minute I set
eyes on you I felt the vibrations, and when
I kissed you——' he stroked her arm '—I was
hooked.'

'And me.' Gabrielle murmured. 'And
me.' Suddenly her brow crinkled. 'Your
idea of franchises, was it decided ages
ago?'

'No. It was only when I saw how dedicated you
were to grinding yourself down into the ground
that I scouted around for ways of releasing you. I
admit that I hadn't spelled out why, but somehow I

knew it wouldn't suit me to have you working sixteen hours a day.'

'And Mrs O'Connor won't,' she assured him. She drained her glass. 'Our house,' she said, 'can it be in the country?'

'Yes.'

'With lots of space?'

'Yes.'

'And we could have a dog?'

'Yes.'

'And trees to climb?'

Saul looked at her in amusement. 'I know I talked about kicking up leaves, but I didn't reckon on you going the whole hog and scaling trees, as well.'

'I won't be.' Gabrielle interlaced her fingers with his. 'But I thought climbing might appeal to a little boy with red hair and blue eyes.'

'A spunky kid?'

'And his brothers and sisters.'

Saul's eyes were moist. 'Oh, yes, sugar,' he murmured. 'Oh, yes.'

2 NEW TITLES FOR JANUARY 1990

Mariah by Sandra Canfield is the first novel in a sensational quartet of sisters in search of love… Mariah's sensual and provocative behaviour contrasts enigmatically with her innocent and naive appearance… Only the maverick preacher can recognise her true character and show her the way to independence and true love.

£2.99

Faye is determined to make a success of the farm she has inherited – but she hadn't accounted for the bitter battle with neighbour, Seth Carradine, who was after the land himself. In desperation she turns to him for help, and an interesting bargain is struck. **Kentucky Woman** by Casey Douglas, bestselling author of Season of Enchantment. **£2.99**

A Mother's Day Treat

This beautifully packaged set of 4 brand new Romances makes an ideal choice of Mother's Day gift.

BLUEBIRDS IN THE SPRING
Jeanne Allen
THE ONLY MAN
Rosemary Hammond
MUTUAL ATTRACTION
Margaret Mayo
RUNAWAY
Kate Walker

These top authors have been selected for their blend of styles, and with romance the key ingredient to all the storylines, what better way to treat your mother... or even yourself.

Available from February 1990.
Price £5.40

From: Boots, Martins, John Menzies, W.H. Smith, Woolworths and other paperback stockists.

SOLITAIRE – Lisa Gregory   £3.50

Emptiness and heartache lay behind the facade of Jennifer Taylor's
glittering Hollywood career. Bitter betrayal had driven her to
become a successful actress, but now at the top, where else
could she go?

SWEET SUMMER HEAT – Katherine Burton   £2.99

Rebecca Whitney has a great future ahead of her until a sultry
encounter with a former lover leaves her devastated...

THE LIGHT FANTASTIC – Peggy Nicholson   £2.99

In this debut novel, Peggy Nicholson focuses on her own
profession... Award-winning author Tripp Wetherby's fear of
flying could ruin the promotional tour for his latest blockbuster.
Rennie Markell is employed to cure his phobia, whatever it takes!

These three new titles will be out in bookshops from February 1990.

W RLDWIDE

TASTY FOOD COMPETITION!

How would you like a years supply of Mills & Boon Romances ABSOLUTELY FREE? Well, you can win them! All you have to do is complete the word puzzle below and send it in to us by March. 31st. 1990. The first 5 correct entries picked out of the bag after that date will win **a years supply of Mills & Boon Romances** (*ten books every month - worth £162*) What could be easier?

```
H O L L A N D A I S E R
E Y E G G O W H A O H A
R S E E C L A I R U C T
B T K K A E T S I F I A
E E T I S M A L C F U T
U R C M T L H E E L Q O
G S I U T F O N O E D U
N H L S O T O N E F M I
I S R S O M A C W A A L
R I A E E T I R J A E L
E F G L L P T O T V R E
M O U S S E E O D O C P
```

CLAM	HOLLANDAISE	OYSTERS	SPICE
COD	JAM	PRAWN	STEAK
CREAM	LEEK	QUICHE	TART
ECLAIR	LEMON	RATATOUILLE	
EGG	MELON	RICE	**PLEASE TURN**
FISH	MERINGUE	RISOTTO	**OVER FOR**
GARLIC	MOUSSE	SALT	**DETAILS**
HERB	MUSSELS	SOUFFLE	**ON HOW**
			TO ENTER

HOW TO ENTER

All the words listed overleaf, below the word puzzle, are hidden in the grid. You can find them by reading the letters forward, backwards, up or down, or diagonally. When you find a word, circle it or put a line through it, the remaining letters (which you can read from left to right, from the top of the puzzle through to the bottom) will ask a romantic question.

After you have filled in all the words, don't forget to fill in your name and address in the space provided and pop this page in an envelope (you don't need a stamp) and post it today. Hurry - competition ends March 31st 1990.

Mills & Boon Competition,
FREEPOST,
P.O. Box 236,
Croydon,
Surrey. CR9 9EL
Only one entry per household

Hidden Question _____

_____

Name _____

Address _____

_____

_____

_____ Postcode _____

COMP 8